ELVIS
And His Friends

Translated from the Swedish
by Sheila La Farge

Illustrated by Harald Gripe

In this sequel to *Elvis and His Secret*,
Elvis is taken to school for the first time
by his mother who wants to show off her
new coat. At roll call he wets his pants.
Even more humiliating, because of his
name, he cannot sing. After watching
Elvis Presley on TV, his mother trims
Elvis' hair like her hero's. Elvis chops off
his bangs in disgust and after the third
day he leaves school. When he decides
to return, he makes a new friend, Annarosa, who lives with her unmarried
mother, grandmother, and great grandmother, and Elvis finds comfort in this
relaxed, unusual family. By the end of
the book, Elvis has grown in understanding and independence of spirit, and
both he and the reader learn to feel
compassion for his insecure, materialistic
mother.

008-0012

Elvis
And His Friends

Elvis
And His Friends

by *MARIA GRIPE*

WITH DRAWINGS BY
Harald Gripe

Translated from the Swedish by
Sheila La Farge

A *Merloyd Lawrence Book*

DELACORTE PRESS/SEYMOUR LAWRENCE

Originally published in Swedish by
Albert Bonniers Förlag, Stockholm, under the title ELVIS! ELVIS!
Copyright © 1973 by Maria Gripe
English translation copyright © 1976
by Dell Publishing Co., Inc.
All rights reserved.
No part of this book may be reproduced in any form
or by any means without the
prior written permission of the Publisher,
excepting brief quotes used in connection with
reviews written specifically for
inclusion in a magazine or newspaper.
Manufactured in the United States of America
First American printing

Library of Congress Cataloging in Publication Data

Gripe, Maria, 1923–
  Elvis and his friends.

  Translation of Elvis! Elvis!
  Sequel to Elvis and His Secret.
  "A Merloyd Lawrence book."
  SUMMARY: With very little help from his interfering
parents, six-year-old Elvis adjusts to starting school and
finally figures out how to handle his mother.
  [1. Parents and child—Fiction.   2. Sweden—Fiction]
I. Gripe, Harald, 1921–   II. Title.
PZ7.G8875EK3   [Fic]   75-8002
ISBN 0-440-02272-X
ISBN 0-440-02273-8 lib. bdg.

JOHN GOULD FLETCHER
  BRANCH LIBRARY
LITTLE ROCK, ARK.

ELVIS AND HIS FRIENDS

CHAPTER

I

Disaster had struck again.

Mom was holding the pieces of broken glass, talking. And talking.

"How many times have I told you to *ask* for a glass when you want a drink? Haven't I told you? At least a hundred times?"

"Yes."

That was true; she said it so often that Elvis forgot to listen.

"Pure disobedience."

Mom stared hard into his eyes.

"You know perfectly well that you're not allowed in the kitchen cupboard by yourself, because accidents like this happen every time you do. You're so clumsy. A real butterfingers! You sure were born under an unlucky star! Weren't you?"

Elvis just stood there. He tried to answer "yes" and

"sure" and "no" in all the right places. It was all he could do. Now Mom wanted him to agree that he was born under an unlucky star; she always wanted him to say that.

"Elvis, you're an ill-starred bird," she said.

That sounded awful. Birds sing and fly. He didn't know anything about ill-starred birds, but they were probably turned to stone. He remembered that once, displayed in a shop window among a lot of bowls, he'd seen a little dark figure with stiff wings. He only saw it for a second; it was so very sad that he didn't want to look at it any more. He realized that it was the ill-starred bird.

He felt like that right now. Breaking things was the most awful feeling. It was like falling to pieces inside; it cut and hurt inside so that he hardly dared breathe.

Then Mom's upset face—and the sound of her crying. She could remember so many things that he had broken.

The sugar bowl with the gold rim, the two coffee cups with roses painted on them, the butter dish Aunt Elsa gave her, the little blue vase that she used for cowslips in springtime. Now she had nothing to put her cowslips in.

"My favorite flowers," she sighed, "where will I put them now?"

This tore Elvis up inside. And the milk mug—remember?—the milk mug she used when she was a baby and kept all her life, until he came along and smashed it.

"There's no way to keep things safe from you, no peace with you around," Mom complained, looking at the slivers of glass in her hand.

"Dad can probably mend the glass," Elvis said.

How could he be so dumb? No one can mend a crystal glass. No, they had to throw it out. Mom tossed the pieces into the garbage fiercely. A sob burst out of Elvis.

"I'll buy you a new one!" he said.

"You can't," said Mom. "They don't make that kind of glass any more. It was a wedding present from my mother. And just think what she'll say when she hears about this . . . she won't like it at all . . . poor Grandma.

"But what can I expect, with someone like you around the house? One thing after another smashed to bits. Soon I won't have a single wedding present left. . . ."

Now that was an exaggeration. The house was full of wedding presents; Mom was always dusting, washing, hanging them out to dry. Elvis said that she didn't have to worry—there were plenty left.

Then Mom started sobbing.

"If only you'd stop defending yourself," she sobbed.

But he wasn't defending himself; he was just trying to make her feel better. But she was not going to feel better—or make him feel better either.

Mom dried her tears and looked at the broken glass in the trash. Then she looked at Elvis and he could hardly bear the way she looked.

He stood absolutely still, and said nothing.

If only he could figure out how it had happened! He had opened the cupboard to get himself an ordinary glass. Then this special one fell out. By itself. He didn't touch it. But it was no good trying to explain that. It never did any good to explain an accident. He could never simply tell what happened because then Mom thought that he was lying. He would have to invent something with lots of words. Then she'd believe him.

But he couldn't do that. He'd never been able to explain himself except by keeping quiet.

It was a shame, because Mom liked words. But Elvis couldn't find any to use—if he did, they never suited Mom; their words never fitted together; they only clashed against each other. So it was better to say nothing.

Mom was talking again, saying that he was ruining them. This meant that he would make them poor. But he'd seen really poor people on TV. They lived very far away; they didn't have any food and almost no clothes. They didn't have decent houses to live in either. It was hard to see how Mom and Dad were going to get poor because their wedding presents were breaking.

He tried to listen to what she was saying. This time he definitely wanted, once and for all, to get a clear idea of why it was so terrible to break wedding presents. Listening to her, he found out why.

That was it—they cost a lot of money! Yes, now he understood. Now he knew why. Mom and Dad were always talking about how their money was running out:

"You've got to have money, otherwise you can't live. Everything costs money. You have to pay for every single little thing in life."

Except for wedding presents. You're given them

when you get married. *Other people* pay for them. Mom didn't have to dip into her *hard-earned savings*. That was why she got so much pleasure out of them. Breaking wedding presents was the same thing as *wasting money*. Now he knew.

Grandad wasted money too. But he did it by buying "fifths" at the store and drinking them. Grandad and Elvis were both destructive money wasters.

He was really glad there was someone else. When he thought of Grandad, he felt a little better. He wasn't alone in his wastefulness, there was perhaps some small comfort in that; and Grandad had lived his whole life buying fifths and still wasn't poor. So Mom really didn't have to be quite so anxious.

But he couldn't explain that to her either. She was always very worried about money; it nearly gave her a heart attack.

That was terribly sad.

And Elvis was expensive too. . . . Well, not himself, he actually came almost free, but everything he wore— now that he could no longer inherit clothes from his uncle Johan—and everything he ate all cost money. In fact, he realized that they could scarcely afford him.

He had a piggy bank that Granny had given him; it was round and fat and rather nice, but its big black eyes didn't look really happy. That was because of all the money they always stuffed into it, and because Mom said that nothing was worth anything except money. But the piggy bank was worth more to Elvis than the money; he wouldn't even mind if it were empty.

He fetched the piggy bank and fiddled with the plastic plug in its tummy. Then he emptied out all the money on the kitchen table.

"Here! You can have all this!" he said to Mom.

The money rolled in all directions. Over the edge of the table and down onto the floor. Under the sofa and behind the stove. One loud, cheery jingling!

This ought to make her very happy!

But she didn't want the money.

"The way you behave!" she shouted furiously, hunting for the coins. Elvis had to help her. And then he had to put all the coins back in the piggy bank again, every single penny. She stood over him, watching. Then she took the piggy bank and put it on a high shelf out of his reach.

"There! You have no understanding of money at all! Or of the value of money, Elvis!" she said.

But he really did. He'd finally figured out what it was all about.

Didn't she realize that?

Later when Mom had gone out shopping, Elvis got a chance to use the phone.

"Now I've wasted money again," he told Grandad.

He sounded like Dad when he was telling how "the gang," which meant his team, had lost against "the ball club."

"Really?" replied Grandad. "On what?"

"A wedding present," said Elvis.

"What?" Grandad sounded surprised. He thought that Elvis had gone out and bought a wedding present for someone and he wondered who was getting married.

"No, for heaven's sake," said Elvis in Dad's tone of voice. "I smashed it, of course."

"How did that happen?" Grandad asked.

"Bad luck again!" said Elvis, like Dad. "Damn bad luck!"

"I see," replied Grandad. "It happens to the best of us."

"It gets worse and worse," said Elvis gloomily. Now he didn't sound like Dad any more. Dad could blame the whole team, eleven men, but Elvis only had himself.

A feeling of hopelessness came over him again. He'd thought that Grandad would say that he had wasted a lot of money in his lifetime too. But Grandad didn't say anything. Elvis had to ask him that himself.

"Sure, sure I have," Grandad answered calmly and firmly as if it were nothing.

"How much have you wasted?" asked Elvis.

"Well, I'll tell you, I don't bother to worry about that," said Grandad. "No use crying over spilt milk. . . ."

"Milk?" said Elvis, astonished. "I thought fifths were liquor!"

Then Grandad burst out laughing. He thought Elvis was very funny.

But Elvis was still perfectly serious. Suddenly he realized that everything was different for Grandad anyway, because he wasted his own money that he had earned himself. Elvis, after all, wasted *other people's* money. Mom and Dad's.

He started talking about something else to avoid thinking about the disaster. And the conversation with Grandad was as much fun as ever. But something still stayed deep inside him, this and all the other accidents he could never forget.

Mom couldn't possibly forget them either. He knew that for sure.

CHAPTER

2

TODAY MOM had to get all dressed up, because today Elvis was starting school, and Mom would go with him. She ran back and forth between the mirror in the hall and the mirror in the bathroom. She could see her whole self in the hall mirror, how she looked in her coat, and in the bathroom mirror she could take a close look to make sure there were no booboos on her face.

Elvis sat waiting for her to be ready. He was all set to go. She had started by fixing him up. He watched her every movement with wonder and alarm. Beforehand, she had chatted with her friends on the phone for a long time about what she should wear, what their opinion was, because it wasn't easy to know what would be most suitable for a day like this.

Now, at least, it had been decided.

Mom would wear her new coat that cost one hundred and twenty-five dollars, but she had bought it at a summer sale at less than half price for fifty-five. There'd been lots of discussions about that coat all through last summer. Dad thought it was too expensive even though it was on sale; he wanted to buy a color TV on the installment plan instead, so he could watch all the championship soccer matches in color. Finally Mom had to borrow the money from Grandma to buy the coat, but they didn't get a color TV anyway —just more discussions.

Mom hadn't had an occasion to wear the coat yet; it had been a little too dressy, but today she would wear it. Because he was going to start school! He felt quite anxious.

He sat quietly and solemnly trying to think. . . .

The fact of the matter was—as Grandad would say— that Elvis had been outwitted. He hadn't been sufficiently alert this time.

Mom had blabbed on and on about school—both as something to be afraid of and something to look forward to—but he never listened. She was always talking too much. Not until it was decided that she should wear the coat did it suddenly dawn on him what was about to happen, and that it would happen to him. He'd never thought about school seriously before. But now, when he saw the coat brought out of the closet, he suddenly realized the enormity of what was happening that day. He, Elvis, was going to start school!

Mom stood there looking at the coat, brushing it a bit. She took it carefully off the hanger, lifted it and slipped it on slowly, straightened the collar. It struck Elvis that the coat looked ordinary, and yet it wasn't. Now he could see that.

Mom twisted and turned in front of the mirror. She was standing under the ceiling light, which was lit, even though it was daytime.

Elvis could see the coat from all sides: from where he sat, he could see the back of the coat right in front of him and the front side in the mirror. A gloomy sight promising bad luck. Mom wasn't pleased with it either.

"I don't get it! I thought it fitted better before. Do you think I've gained weight?" she asked.

Elvis didn't know. She had tried on the coat before, several times, when he wasn't watching. Now there was no doubt about it: this was one of those typical coats that mothers put on when kids start school.

"Ugh, I'm no beauty today, no matter what I do," Mom sighed.

Elvis agreed with her but said nothing.

She tried a scarf around her neck; it looked better, she said. Then she tried another and that was even better, though she still wondered whether she shouldn't have bought another coat instead—the green one that Gun-Britt liked. Now she would have to put up with this one for ever and ever, she said to the mirror; she was so unlucky with everything. . . .

Elvis knew that. With him, for example—she didn't say it but he had known for ages how maddening it was that he came along and not a girl. Girls are definitely so much more fun to dress.

Suddenly Mom turned around and asked if he had peed.

He squirmed and got down from the chair. Yes, he had peed.

"Are you sure?"

She turned off the hall light and the radio. Yes, he was sure, he didn't have to.

"Okay, then we're all set."

Elvis stood there motionless. The sun shone into the rooms. It was still and quiet. Princess lay in the kitchen, Mom's "precious little sweetheart," sleeping in her basket. Mom tidied her hair in front of the mirror; Elvis watched her; their eyes met in the mirror.

"Shall we go?" she asked.

He moved his eyes from hers and looked around.

Sunlight shone on the thresholds. They glowed exactly like gold. The sight of this would have made him happy on any other day. The thresholds were the very best things they had at home. When he was away and homesick, he thought of them, their sun thresholds.

"Then let's go," Mom repeated.

She walked toward the door. Elvis went slowly after her. There was nothing else he could do. He had given up. Usually he was right on his toes, but this time he hadn't slipped away early enough, so all he could do was go along with her.

When he came home, he probably would be quite different, not like himself. He would be a *schoolchild*. And he knew all about them. He had seen them. A totally different kind of human being.

Instinctively he grabbed an old umbrella standing in the hall. Mom instantly took it away from him.

"What do you want that for? The sun is shining!"

She slammed their door. Soon after, the outside door closed behind them too.

They started walking.

There was no turning back.

Mom walked first.

Elvis followed her.

After a while she stopped and took his hand. Just for a second . . . but she was wearing white gloves! And Elvis' hands . . . you never know . . . of course, he scrubbed himself properly so that he'd be really clean, but still . . . maybe it was risky. Because Elvis was always Elvis. And white is white. So then Mom walked ahead of him again, and Elvis had to trot along after the coat and gloves all the way to school.

At every shop window they passed, Mom slowed down to look at her reflection.

"I think I'll do!" she said to Elvis. "At least you don't have to be ashamed of me."

What was she saying now?

Elvis was so astounded that he stopped right where he was in the middle of the thoroughfare. *He* would be ashamed of Mom? Wasn't she the one who was always ashamed of him?

"Hurry up! You'll get run over!" Mom shouted from the sidewalk.

She looked impatient. No, he obviously hadn't heard her correctly. . . .

Now the school building came into sight. They would soon be there. From every direction, lots of mothers and their kids were gathering. Mom stopped and looked. Then she looked down and caught sight of Elvis' hands. She chose the one that looked cleaner and walked the last bit of the way holding his hand.

"Don't you think all the mothers and their kids look nice walking hand in hand?" she said looking around, smiling.

But Elvis had stopped thinking; he just let his legs take him wherever they wanted. No thoughts were stirring in his head any more.

Mom was terribly pleased by it all. This is really going well, she was thinking, perhaps he isn't quite as impossible as he often seems. It'll be good for him to start school now. She'd never seen him so easy to get on with before. Really nice.

She looked around, nodded and smiled. Caught other people's smiles. Tried to talk with Elvis, tried to say encouraging things about what they were doing. She listened and copied the other mothers. She wanted to feel like them.

"What a fine big schoolyard, Elvis! Have you looked at it? This is where you'll play during recess. You'll have lots of fun friends. Look around!"

She was having a good time and feeling fine in her coat. She thought that the others were looking at it. She was enjoying taking Elvis to start school. She squeezed his hand.

"Yes sir, Elvis, this is a big day!"

Then they walked into the school building. It was cool inside and full of echoes, but the air was gray. Elvis simply went along with her. Mom started talking with the other mothers.

"My Gunnar has so looked forward to today," one of them said.

"So has my Elvis," said Mom.

And Elvis didn't contradict her. His will had shrunk down inside him to a tiny, wrinkly raisin. He could already feel how he was changing into a schoolboy. It was as if he had been knocked unconscious and hardly noticed what was happening around him.

Now they found someone who must be the teacher, and the two women walked into her classroom, taking him along. So there he was, standing there. Mom talked to the teacher. Elvis didn't look at either of them. And he didn't hear what they were saying.

He realized they were talking about him, because he heard his name mentioned. He didn't care about what they were saying. They laughed too, strange little laughs. Mom shook him gently, laughed again!

Something like eternity passed, lots of time running out, and suddenly he noticed that he was sitting at a school desk.

And the sun was really shining. . . .

It shone on the desk top so that it glowed just like the thresholds at home. How great the desk smelled, warmed by the sun. The wood was smooth on top and rough underneath. It was a good desk.

The air in the room was no longer gray, it was lighter; and he didn't feel so dim and dull inside.

But where was Mom? Her coat and gloves, where were they?

Lots of mothers were standing along the wall but he didn't want to look over in that direction. Mom had better be paying attention to him, so that he wouldn't get lost here in the middle of everything. School seemed to be full of commotion.

What were they up to now? Someone was calling out names somewhere! And after every name someone else answered "yes." What was the point of that? No one was doing anything. They were just sitting there! And the mothers were standing! Strange school. How long would this go on?

Oh oh—he discovered that he had to pee. He had to pee terribly badly.

Obviously he had to hold on. This usually worked out all right; he was often quite busy with something else when he felt he had to pee, so he was used to holding on. For quite a long time.

But it was one thing to be busy and working hard, and quite another to be just sitting. And sitting. With nothing happening. Only a lot of blabbering.

Suddenly someone said:

"Elvis Karlsson."

What now?

Elvis concentrated on his desk top. He had no desire to look up. They would have to figure it all out without him. . . .

"Elvis! Didn't you hear? The teacher called you!" he heard Mom say.

Holy mackerel! He had to pee so badly.

What were they up to? Why couldn't they all stop blabbing?

Oh oh, oops—there it goes. . . .

It started coming and dribbled down on him. It smelled and dripped on the floor.

The coat and the gloves suddenly appeared beside him.

Then he couldn't remember any more.

The dimness in his head returned, so that he didn't remember how it all ended. Only that they had to take a taxi home.

And then, of course, there were lots of discussions later. . . .

"Didn't I tell you? Didn't I tell you to pee before we left home? Imagine—peeing in your pants on the first day of school! And during roll call! What will people think?"

What happened was discussed over and over. The friends on the phone thought that Elvis was very nervous in school and that was why he couldn't hold on.

Ridiculous! He wasn't nervous about school at all.

Besides, nervous was a typical word that her friends on the phone used all the time.

Why should he be frightened of school? After all, they didn't do anything there. Nothing happened the whole time. And he wasn't going to turn into a school-child either. He could feel that he was still the same. The change hadn't come over him.

But, if he went there again, well, time would tell. It was something he had to think about.

When Mom finished phoning and went out for a while, Elvis dialed Grandad. He had promised the day before to call as soon as he could and tell Grandad what happened in school.

"Well?" asked Grandad. "How did it go?"

"The fact of the matter is I peed in my pants," said Elvis.

"You did?" said Grandad. "Was it okay?"

"Fine, but Mom got a little on her coat when she was wiping it up," Elvis told him.

"That was sloppy! What did she do?"

"You see, she didn't notice that it had dripped on the seat."

"She should be a bit more careful next time," said Grandad. "She's usually very neat and tidy, so she won't do it again."

Elvis didn't think she would either.

"What will people think?" he asked anxiously.

"People?" Grandad wondered.

"Yes. *People,*" repeated Elvis.

"What they think has nothing to do with you at all," said Grandad.

"Nope, that's true . . . but still, what will they say?" Elvis wondered again.

"That's their business," Grandad thought. Elvis needn't bother himself about it. Let people think and say whatever they want to.

Sure, Elvis agreed with that. In fact, it wasn't anything to get too worked up about.

"Did anything else happen in school?" Grandad asked.

"Not that I can remember," Elvis said.

"What about the teacher? Did you like her?"

But Elvis couldn't remember her either. He had scarcely looked at her. But:

"There was sunlight on the desk!" he remembered suddenly.

"That's not bad!" said Grandad.

"Though, of course, you know I won't be going there any more."

There was silence at the other end of the phone for a moment. Then Grandad asked whether Elvis thought that was wise.

"What do you think?" Elvis asked.

"I think you ought to find out what the teacher looks like," answered Grandad. "I think you should, before you really make up your mind for good."

"You think so?"

"Obviously you can't give up school before you know what kind of teacher you have. Or at least I wouldn't," said Grandad decisively. "I'm not that stupid."

No, of course, maybe he could go there just once more, just to take a little look. . . .

"But I don't intend to be a schoolchild, see," he said.

No risk of that, according to Grandad. Elvis was sure to go on being just the same.

And Mom thought so too, but said it in her way.

"Count on you, Elvis," she said that evening. "It never fails."

She was carrying on about her coat, he could tell. The spot had been removed, but she intended to discuss it some more anyway. He knew that.

She wasn't going to forget that he had peed on himself the very first day in school. Grandad forgot things like that right away, because he had other, more important things to think about.

And so did Peter. He knew lots of people who had peed in their pants. It wasn't at all because of being nervous or scared of school. It's just impossible to hold on endlessly, indefinitely. It was as simple as that.

If only Mom could hear what Peter and Grandad said instead of listening to those blabbermouths on the phone all the time.

CHAPTER

3

WHAT ABOUT SCHOOL, really? Was there anything in it for him?

He no longer believed that he would change into a schoolchild. He'd figured that out, because Mom's friends had kids who went to school, and of course, there'd been lots of talk about them, with Mom always saying exactly the same thing:

"You'll see, Elvis, school will put an end to all this. You won't be able to be the way you are, you'll have to behave yourself."

It sounded as if you turned into something very particular the minute you started school. But now he knew for sure that he was himself, and that he'd decide for himself whether he wanted to change in some way or other. If he wanted to, then he would, but *by himself* in that case. And of course, he didn't want to, so that wasn't the point.

And yet . . . if he wasn't good enough the way he was—and now, after that business of peeing, people quite possibly wouldn't think that he was—what should he do?

That was the main thing he was worried about.

So what should he do?

Heck—he might as well go along with school. . . .

He didn't know any other way—because if he wasn't good enough, then quite obviously school wasn't the place for him, so they'd have to do without him there.

Maybe that was just as well?

He mulled it over and over, but he didn't let on about it to Mom. And the next morning when he was supposed to go off, he didn't let on either, even though he'd almost decided not to go to school.

Mom had bought him a schoolbag and lots of school things. They wouldn't be thrown out, because he could definitely get some use out of all of it anyway.

"Are you really sure you can find your way now?" Mom asked when he was ready to leave. "Don't you want me to go along with you to make sure?"

No, it wasn't necessary. He'd find his way.

But he had to go to the toilet once more, for safety's sake.

"So you don't repeat yesterday's accident again today," she said.

Nothing came, not a drop, but Mom was reassured, and finally he was on his way.

She stood at the window watching him go, and he heard her shout as usual: ·

"Elvis! ELVIS!"

He didn't usually bother when she shouted out the window, but since he wasn't going to school, he stopped and listened to what she wanted.

"Remember to ask for Miss Magnusson's class, Elvis, if you can't find the right room. Can you remember that now? Your teacher's name is Miss Magnusson. And come straight home after school, do you hear?"

Elvis nodded. This was starting to get embarrassing. How could he do that?

The school was not far. He had nothing special to do right now, so he really wouldn't be losing any time if he went that way. After all, he didn't have to go in, just walk by the school building. And he could take a look around. . . .

The schoolyard was full of kids.

Once a whole lot of schoolchildren had attacked him and hit him with their schoolbags, but that was long ago; now he had a schoolbag too.

He stopped awhile and watched. If they attacked him, all he had to do was run away.

But no one came. No one even looked in his direction. He stood there for a long while, but no, they didn't pay any attention to him at all. They treated him like the empty air.

A couple of boys walked past him on the street. When they went in through the school gates, Elvis simply followed along. Now he was inside the yard!

It was as easy as pie! He hadn't thought that he could follow along so simply.

But—he still had his freedom. All he had to do was walk out again. . . .

He walked around on the packed earth of the schoolyard, and nothing happened.

Crowds of kids were milling around, walking, standing, running, but no one paid any attention to him. Not a single person.

Would they discover him soon?

Or had he become invisible?

He had almost walked around the whole schoolyard without being noticed.

In a way it was good, but not in another way.

It was good, because he could think in peace even though there were so many people around, packed in like sardines. But if you happened to want to chat with someone, then it wasn't too good. Not that he wanted to, but anyway. . . .

No, there was no point going inside with all of them when the bell rang. Besides, it was a cloudy day, so no sunshine would be making the desk top glow. It was probably just plain gray inside.

Might as well head off right away.

He started walking hurriedly toward the school

gates. Then two girls came rushing toward him at full speed. One of them was chasing the other, yelling and shrieking. They didn't see him but ran right into him, so that he toppled over, spread-eagle, his schoolbag and his cap flying every which way.

The girls dashed on without paying any attention to him. He picked himself up and found his cap, but he couldn't see his schoolbag. Where could it have gone? Close by, there was a bunch of kids, but he didn't dare ask if they'd seen his bag. He just stood staring. All he wanted was to be somewhere else instantly, but he couldn't leave without his schoolbag.

What was wrong with him anyway? Suddenly he was furious with himself. Here he was, feeling insecure. Terribly anxious. Why? Yes, well, because his schoolbag was missing. Just as if there were a secret power inside it. He felt as if he wouldn't be able to protect himself if any kids attacked him now the way they did that time they hit him with their schoolbags.

Ridiculous! That was ages ago, when he was little and didn't understand anything. Before he knew that he was alone—really alone.

But now, after all, he knew that he had himself; now he could deal with people who saw him and also people who didn't.

In fact, it didn't matter one way or the other whether he went or stayed. It was all the same, really.

But he wanted his schoolbag back. Then he could do what he liked.

If only he could find out where it had gone!

He had to get it before the bell rang because then everyone would go into the school building. They'd disappear in all directions and it would be more difficult to find. He had to sharpen his wits now. It must have ended up somewhere.

Anyway, he was pleased that he wasn't frightened any more and that he could think things over and discuss them with himself.

He took a turn around the schoolyard; things didn't look too hopeful. But how could something simply vanish? It was a mystery.

Then he heard a voice behind him:

"Is this your bag?"

He turned around. A girl was standing there with his schoolbag.

"I saw you lose it," she said.

She explained that she had picked it up because he didn't.

"You just stood there staring; you didn't see it," she said, acting out for Elvis how he had been standing. But she wasn't laughing at him.

Elvis took his bag and the girl stayed there.

"I have one just like yours," she said, showing him her bag.

Yes, he could see it was the same. She opened her bag and took out a big old atlas with a blue cover and

a big picture of the world right in the middle. Elvis recognized the world, but this one was yellow; on TV it was usually gray.

"Not on color TV and not when the sun shines on it," said the girl.

Elvis explained that they didn't have a color TV because they had bought a coat instead. And then she said that they didn't have one either, but she had seen a color TV at someone else's house.

"Are we all supposed to have atlases like that?" Elvis asked. "I don't have one."

The girl shook her head. She didn't know. She had

to ask the teacher whether they were going to need atlases in school. She had just borrowed this one, but she might be given it some day.

"It belongs to Old Granny," she said. "She's going to die soon."

"She is?" said Elvis, terrified. "Is she ill?"

"Oh no, just old."

The atlas was valuable, she explained solemnly, putting it back in her schoolbag. It cost a lot, so she had to take good care of it.

"What do you have in your schoolbag? Can I see?" she asked.

Elvis showed her the school things that his mom had bought him. She thought they were fine; she wanted things just like his.

But Elvis didn't think they were as good as her atlas at all. With something like that, you didn't need a whole lot of school things. She agreed, but Old Granny had said that the teacher would decide.

She looked around the schoolyard; her eyes stopped when they reached the school building.

"It's so big," she said. "I'll never find my classroom."

"I will!" said Elvis without thinking, deciding right then that he was going inside the building too. He might as well, since he was there.

He said, "I'll show you the way."

"Maybe we aren't in the same class. You know, there're so many classes," she said, worrying.

"I'll find it anyway!"

Of course, he didn't remember much at all about what the inside of the building looked like, he had been so out of it the day before; but she looked him right in the eye in a way that made him feel absolutely confident. Because she trusted what he said. She took him at his word. Yes, now he would see to it that she got to her class. And they had to be in the same room since her teacher's name was Miss Magnusson too.

"I didn't see you yesterday," she said. "Did you see me?"

Elvis shook his head—he would have liked to say that he had seen her, but in fact, he hadn't.

"I didn't see anyone yesterday," he said by way of an explanation.

"You must have seen the boy who peed," she said.

Elvis opened his eyes wide; he was startled and confused.

"But that was me!" he said.

Didn't she recognize him? How dumb of him to say anything. Her eyes were very round as she looked at him doubtingly.

"Really?" she asked.

Yes. Elvis nodded. Definitely. He was the one.

"How did you dare? I would have died. . . ."

"Heck," said Elvis, "it was nothing. . . ."

"Yes, but. . . ."

"You can't always hold on for ever and ever," he explained.

"No, but. . . ."

"The fact of the matter is that you can't," he said.

She wasn't about to burst into laughter, she wasn't shocked; she just looked at him intently, steadily, in a way that he wasn't used to, that made him happy.

Just then the bell rang.

Everyone ran toward the school door. It turned out that they had no trouble finding their way. Miss Magnusson was standing inside by the stairs waiting, and she remembered everyone in her class. Even Elvis. But he hadn't looked at her yesterday, so she must have looked at him. She even remembered his name.

"Welcome, Elvis," she said. "And welcome, Annarosa."

Annarosa? Of course . . . the girl next to him, that was her name.

As soon as she saw the teacher, she opened her schoolbag and pulled out the atlas again.

"That's really nice," said the teacher. "I'll look at it later."

"No, now!" Annarosa explained that Old Granny wanted to know right away whether they would use it in school, because it was worth a lot of money.

Miss Magnusson took the book, looked inside it and carefully leafed through the pages, while everyone else in the class crowded around to see it too.

"It's really very fine, and old; it was printed in 1887," Miss Magnusson said. "Very nice."

"What do you think it is worth?" Annarosa asked.

Old Granny wanted her to ask that, and Miss Magnusson leafed in the book again but shook her head. She didn't know.

"But it's much too good to have in school," she said, returning the book to Annarosa.

"Oh no. I can have it, if I look after it," Annarosa answered eagerly. She handed the book back to Miss Magnusson. "Look, it has such beautiful colors! Of course I need it in school."

Miss Magnusson looked thoughtful; she leafed through the book again, but Elvis noticed that she didn't really look at it; she just turned the pages, here and there, and bit her lip.

"Unfortunately you won't get much use out of it in school," she said at last. "You see, the world doesn't look like this any more. The world looks very different today."

She closed the book briskly and gave it back. Then she entered her classroom and all the kids followed her. No one thought about the atlas any more.

Annarosa fumbled as she put it back in her schoolbag, and Elvis helped her. He looked somewhat fearfully at the picture of the glowing world. It didn't look like that any more? Then what did it look like now?

CHAPTER

4

THE WHOLE FIRST DAY Elvis went to school.

And the whole second day.

And the third. . . .

But then he didn't go any more.

In fact, he hadn't planned on going at all, but he ended up spending three whole days and didn't regret the time. But there wasn't much for him to do in school. He already knew the alphabet, since he knew how to read. And he could count too—anyway, further than the others—and he also knew how to write.

He might have gone on going to school despite all that, if it hadn't been for the singing.

Because he had a very hoarse voice and couldn't sing. *Didn't want to*, either.

The real Elvis, whose records Mom had at home, knew how to sing, but not Elvis Karlsson. And people who can't sing should be left in peace. But in school he had to, everyone had to in school because the teacher wanted them to.

That was why he stopped going.

Besides, he discovered that she wasn't their *real* teacher. All they had been given was a substitute. The real one wouldn't come until after Christmas, and maybe *one* substitute at a time was plenty, he thought, because in a way he was a kind of substitute himself; you could say that he was a substitute—for the *real* Elvis.

Otherwise there was nothing wrong with Miss Magnusson, she was fine, if only she weren't so crazy about singing. They had to sing every single day. Several times. He certainly hoped their real teacher had other interests. Somehow or other he thought he'd put off school until she came back.

What's more, he couldn't sit where he wanted to! Miss Magnusson always moved him. She wanted him to sit in the same place every day, right in front. Annarosa sat way in the back, and there were lots of other kids in between.

And then all three days were cloudy, so there was no sunlight on the desk top, and Miss Magnusson said it would go on being cloudy now because it was autumn.

And then in recess Annarosa went off with the other girls. They didn't know her, they didn't ask her to come along, but she followed them anyway. They said

the girls should be with the girls and the boys with the
boys. How dumb can you get!

He wanted to be with Annarosa. The boys didn't
know him either and he didn't know them.

Annarosa was by far the smallest and quietest in the
class. She had brown hair, almost exactly his color,
which she wore in two tufts, one by each ear. And her
eyes fitted so well in his. The other kids' eyes didn't,
but he could look into hers as long as he wanted.

So of course, it was a shame to quit school . . . but
what could he do? He couldn't bear the singing.

He didn't tell anyone he was thinking of quitting
when he went home on the third day. No one in
school knew. Not even Annarosa. He thought of telling her, asking her opinion, but she just walked right
past him that day on the way home. She didn't see
him. He stood there waiting, but she was watching the
girl who was in front of her. Then he decided not to
go any more.

He went over to see Peter at home the next day
instead. Mom thought that he was going to school,
because he didn't want to talk with her about the fact
he had quit. That would only make a big discussion
again. But Peter said that he had to talk about it,
because otherwise there would only be more fighting
afterward when they found out about it at home.

But first they made a mushroom expedition in the
woods so they'd be able to talk about it all in peace

and quiet. They rode on Peter's bike. The air was misty and smelled a bit like autumn. It was so quiet in the woods that he could hardly bear to break the silence with a word. Too bad they had to have a discussion!

Peter began talking but Elvis mostly picked mushrooms and thought. And listened to what Peter had to say.

He thought that Elvis should stay home a couple of days and think it all through once more, because sometimes it's dumb to make a decision too fast. When the real teacher came, the others might have got way ahead of Elvis in counting, for example, and then he'd have a problem. The fact that he was ahead now in everything was all to the good, not bad.

Yes, that was true—but the business of singing was something Peter didn't know about, and the fact that Annarosa only wanted to be with the girls. Elvis didn't want to talk about that. Not right now. He had to think it all through himself first.

They made a fire on a slope in the woods and cooked the mushrooms immediately, then ate them by the fire. Peter had brought along everything they needed. Afterward they drank tea that he had also brought in his thermos.

While they were having tea, Peter told Elvis what school had been like for him when he started, and it was interesting because Peter couldn't sit still in those

days. The moment he sat down at his desk, his legs
started itching and twitching so he had to get up and
run. He'd just get going, sometimes right in the middle of class, when his legs started fidgeting. And he
couldn't hear what the teacher said. He heard everything else instead. The tiny little sounds that are always in the background. His hearing was very good

when he was little and his teacher's voice seemed too loud, so loud that he couldn't hear her, he just couldn't manage it. This was difficult, because he didn't learn anything. He wanted to quit school at least a hundred times, but then he didn't, and in the end it got better. He got so that he could sit still and after a while they were taught more interesting things. Maybe it was never really wonderful, but good enough for him to go on and become what he wanted to be. And that was why he went there, so that he could become what he wanted to be. That was why Peter thought that Elvis should wait a while longer before quitting. You never know what might happen. He might change his mind again.

Elvis promised to wait, but he forgot the promise when he got home, stupidly enough, because there was such a big discussion. In the end all he said was that he didn't think he'd go to school any more! And no one could make him! Period, the end!

Then he stopped talking and they couldn't get another word out of him.

Mom phoned around and her friends thought that he was too young, not really ready for school yet. Probably a kid should be seven and Elvis wasn't quite seven yet. He wouldn't be before the end of the year.

Not ready for school. . . . Ridiculous!

He could both read and write! And count—quite far anyway.

Could he be not ready for school just because he didn't want to sing?

Though, of course, he hadn't told Mom about the singing. He knew only too well which old story she would come up with then.

Because once Elvis had sung perfectly.

When he was little. . . .

It happened so suddenly and naturally that he hadn't even noticed it himself: once, when he was sitting on the floor, in the hall, and all around him the sunlight glowed on the thresholds. No one was home. He had got hold of Mom's button box. She'd forgotten to hide it as usual. A big box full of shiny buttons. He took the top off and stirred his index finger around in the buttons. It felt great—and sounded beautiful. Then he emptied out all the buttons on the floor, so that they rolled around. And he made flowers with them all over the floor.

That was when the song came. He heard it and he felt it, though he didn't think about the fact that it was his own voice singing. He thought about the beautiful flowers he was going to make on the floor. The voice floated out in the air effortlessly by itself, like the sunlight. And it was so loud that he didn't hear the key in the lock.

Suddenly there was Mom standing in the midst of the button flowers.

Then the voice stopped.

Mom didn't get angry about her button box, not at

first. She clapped her hands and wanted him to sing some more. He sounded so "sweet," she said, and he wasn't hoarse when he sang. A while later she asked him to sing again when there were guests, Grandma and some ladies. Everyone wanted to hear him. But that voice never returned. It vanished as swiftly as it had come.

And he wasn't allowed to play with the buttons any more.

So it was easy to know what kind of discussion there'd be if she learned that he stopped school to get out of singing. Luckily no one knew. Mom was angry enough as it was.

She was even grumpy with her telephone friends. After all, she could make up her own mind whether Elvis was ready for school. Didn't she know best, his very own "mother"? They talked a lot of nonsense to make themselves more important, she told Dad.

"The child is being pigheaded as usual," she said. "He always has to do the exact opposite of everyone else. He's just like the old man!"

The old man was Grandad.

Dad didn't say much of anything, he mostly mumbled and agreed. At last Mom said that he had to have it out with Elvis, and so then he shouted as usual:

"Now you do what Mom says and go to school tomorrow, Elvis! Get it? Otherwise you'll have me to answer to!"

Then nothing more happened. Mom thought that

he was "a pushover"; she was furious with everyone now, with Dad and Elvis and her phone friends.

But she was angriest at Grandad.

"There's no talking to that old man," she said.

This was because Grandad thought that the whole discussion was unnecessary. He didn't see why Elvis had to start school right now, since he didn't want to and didn't have to. Not until next autumn. There was no hurry, he thought, so why force him?

"Don't I have any say in the matter?" asked Mom.

She wanted Elvis put somewhere for at least a few hours a day so she'd know where he was, and could stop worrying about him, so she wouldn't have to stand hollering at the window.

"Is that too much to ask?"

She was looking forward to having Elvis in school, really looking forward to it, so she'd finally have a little tidiness and order in her house.

"I don't intend to give in this time!" she told Grandad.

Elvis heard that conversation.

Couldn't Mom clean the house even if he didn't go to school? She was always cleaning!

And if *she* didn't intend to give in, then he couldn't either.

No, never!

CHAPTER

5

"Out of the way! I've no time for you now!" Mom said wherever he went.

He was not allowed to get in the way that day, because the color TV was coming. That was why there was such a hurry. Mom had to clean and make everything fine and tidy so they could welcome it properly.

They'd finally decided that they had to have a color TV anyway. There were lots of discussions about it for a long time—many of their friends and several neighbors already had color TVs. Mom didn't want them to end up being the last in the building, so now it was all set: today at four o'clock the color TV was coming.

In plenty of time for the evening program.

Because that evening the *real* Elvis was appearing on TV at eight o'clock. That was why they couldn't wait until Christmas for the color TV the way Dad wanted, which they would have done otherwise. Mom had to see the real Elvis in color. She didn't want to go over to someone else's house to watch him. She wanted to be in her own home.

Elvis would also be allowed to watch him. And Dad too. In just a few hours they could all watch the real Elvis, imagine!

Mom had a big picture of him hanging on the wall, in color too, but it would be quite different to see him moving.

Elvis leapt out of the way of the vacuum cleaner as best he could, but it chased him everywhere. His heart hopped and thumped in his chest. He got excited too. There was a kind of giddy dizziness in the air. It was like when the stranger from Stockholm came right in the middle of spring cleaning, but more solemn and special.

He didn't know what to do with himself. He didn't dare go out either, in case he might lose track of the time.

"What time is it, Mom?" he asked over and over.

Mom didn't answer him any more. She thought he was being a pest. He was and he knew it, but he just had to know. . . . When guests were coming, Mom would say, "They're coming at six o'clock!" But he didn't know when six o'clock was. And Mom made it sound as if the guests were standing outside the door the whole time. He felt uneasy, restless. Sometimes he'd run and hide when they came.

"You'll miss out on a lot that way," Mom said.

Afterward he'd be told, "Mai had some candies for you, Elvis. If you'd been a nice polite boy and said hello to her, she would have given them to you. But now you have nothing."

Just because he didn't say hello! On the whole, this business about guests and candies was a problem: were they bringing something or not? How could you ever know that ahead of time?

He was honestly fed up with all that. You can't run up and say hello to someone just for candies. What if you don't get any? You'd feel so stupid!

Besides, in the long run he felt sort of stupid getting candies anyway. With Mom standing there saying that he had to bow politely and say thank you. And say thanks *himself*! The last time someone came over with candies was really the limit, he felt, so he took the candies and handed them right off to Mom.

After all, they brought the candies for her sake: they actually weren't for him at all. They only gave them to him when she was watching, so she'd think that they were being nice—to Elvis, who was so dumb.

Naturally they wondered what was wrong with him; they thought there was something wrong with the candies, that he didn't like that kind. He didn't say anything. It was no use explaining that kind of thing.

But he felt just like Princess every time; she started yowling as soon as anyone rustled a paper bag out in the kitchen. It was hard to put an end to this sort of thing, especially when Mom said:

"See whether they've brought something for you, Elvis, when they come over this evening."

This would immediately start the candy thoughts going and they would get stuck in his head—even though he knew perfectly well that it was only to persuade him to say hello and make a good impression, as Mom would say.

It was even happening right now! Suddenly he wondered whether the real Elvis was going to bring him something! The air was loaded with just that kind of expectation.

To top it all, the color TV didn't arrive at four as they promised.

They didn't come until half past five. Mom was going out of her mind from worry. She phoned the store and then Dad at work. What if they didn't hook up the TV in time for the program!

At last they got going. The TV arrived at the same time as Dad.

By then Mom had really had it. Elvis too. Dad thought that Elvis had a fever, because he was so hot; his cheeks were like red apples polished for Christmas.

"What have you done to the kid?" he asked Mom. "He looks all worn out."

But Mom hadn't done anything to Elvis. She hadn't had time for him. She looked blankly at Dad.

Elvis said nothing, but in fact, he didn't feel very well. Kind of uneasy in his stomach.

And Dad had other things to think about just then; he had to help with the TV.

Elvis went out into the kitchen and sat with Princess for the moment.

Princess had been in the way all day too. That had never happened before. Mom, who always stood up for her, had snubbed and snapped at her all day. And Princess, who wasn't used to that, whined and howled all afternoon. But now she was sleeping, an uneasy sleep—her body twitched, she was dreaming.

Elvis sat watching her. And he listened to the voices discussing the color TV. Suddenly he shivered and started yawning until the tears rolled out of his eyes. He couldn't stop them.

A little while later he was sleeping too, right next to Princess.

He slept until Dad woke him.

Dad said, "It's time, Elvis!"

Elvis rubbed his eyes. Right! The real Elvis!

They went into the big room.

The ceiling light was turned off.

Mom had lit candles, one on the table by the sofa and one on the record player. She'd poured wine into her glass and Dad's; Dad would have preferred beer, but it wasn't suitable. Elvis was given a soft drink, that was suitable. He was wide awake now. Princess too. She lay on the floor at Mom's feet.

Mom had bought a big bunch of cut flowers, which she'd put in a vase on top of the color TV. Flowers from a florist, expensive ones; Elvis had never planted any like that.

Mom leaned forward eagerly. The program was starting.

There was a great swirl of colors and a tremendous roar of sound.

Then the colors separated. They turned into one huge church with lots of different colored stars up on the ceiling.

And now—Elvis' heart started to beat faster, it even thumped in his ear lobes. He turned red.

ELVIS ELVIS ELVIS

ELVIS was written over the whole sky, written with the stars which lit up and went out and lit up again. In plain huge letters the stars wrote out:

ELVIS ELVIS

It was beautiful and unlike anything he had ever experienced. He felt his throat tighten, his whole face got hot, the roots of his hair tingled.

At the same time it felt a little like when Mom stood at the window shouting Elvis so that you could hear it all over town. He wanted to become invisible, disappear into a hole.

"It's like being in seventh heaven," whispered Mom.

"The picture definition isn't bad, is it?" said Dad.
"And the color's just great!"

On the TV a crowd of people who looked very
weird were waving and gesturing wildly with their
arms and screaming. Now! There! Yes!

Here comes the real ELVIS!

Elvis quickly covered his face with his hands and peeked between his fingers. The sight made him quite upset and giddy. Even though he'd seen plenty of pictures of him, he was just as bewildered by it. And shy. Confused and excited at the same time.

He spread his fingers and had a better look.

Mom and Dad weren't watching him, thank goodness. Mom was completely involved with the TV; Dad was busy with his pipe; and the real ELVIS couldn't see him at all.

"He's got so fat!" said Dad suddenly. "A really fleshy pot. Not exactly the athletic type."

Mom didn't hear what he said, but Elvis did—what did Dad mean, not the athletic type?

"Can't he play soccer?" he asked carefully.

Dad chuckled.

"That one!" he said. "What do you think? With thighs like his! No sir, that's no player."

So? Then maybe it wasn't so strange that Elvis was bad at soccer, since the real one couldn't play either.

But—he could sing, after all. He had started now. Elvis would never be able to sing like that. His singing voice disappeared long ago. . . .

He leaned back into the armchair and watched. He didn't feel quite so shy any more; he started looking around, from Dad to Mom to Princess. But mostly he watched the real ELVIS.

Water was dripping off the real ELVIS' face. Singing looked like sweaty work. A lot of ladies offered him handkerchiefs all at once, so that he could wipe the sweat off. Sometimes he kissed them to say thank you. But then he got just as sweaty right away. It was actually very interesting to see how quickly it happened. He got really soaking wet. The ladies had to take care of him again. A good thing they were there, otherwise it would be too hard work for him.

He had some disciples along too; they wore necklaces and white clothes, but only ELVIS himself wore gold. They played different instruments and sang along, when he told them to. Sometimes they came on with pink and blue scarves, really long ones, which they hung around his neck. They had to give him fresh ones all the time, because he gave them right away to the ladies who helped him with his sweating. But sometimes he wiped himself off on the scarves first. It must have tickled, but still . . . he shouldn't have! Not when there were handkerchiefs around!

Elvis looked at Mom to see what she thought about that—because she was always so particular about those things—but she didn't notice it at all.

She just smiled and sucked on the rim of her wineglass. And rocked to the music. She was happy. Her face was all smooth and calm.

"Great picture," said Dad. "Great, isn't it?"

"Yes, but how can it be colored?" asked Elvis.

"Hush, Elvis!" Mom said.

Dad said that he'd explain later, after the program.

The real ELVIS shone and glowed on the TV, flashes and glitters came from him. Obviously someone like Elvis Karlsson was just trash beside him.

Of course, that was what Mom had discovered. They couldn't be compared. It would be better if she just stopped doing that.

Princess started pawing Mom, demanding to be petted. Mom shoved her away, then Princess barked.

"Leave me alone, Princess!" said Mom.

She moved closer to the TV.

Just then ELVIS wasn't singing; he was talking a weird kind of talk. The ladies were waving their arms in the air and shouting; some got kissed.

"Put the dog out in the kitchen, Olle!" Mom said. "She's driving me crazy."

Dad got up and went out with Princess, who was howling.

When he came back, he repeated that the picture was fine.

"You have to agree. Seldom seen better. This set is much better quality than Ingrid and Gösta's," he said.

"Shush!" said Mom.

ELVIS had started singing again. A serious song. He stood with his disciples around him, just the way Jesus stood with his in Granny's painting, the one over her bed, but that one wasn't in color. Still, they were rather alike, when he thought about it.

They sang *hallelujah*, all together, *glory, glory,*

hallelujah. Elvis heard it distinctly; he remembered the song from Mom's ELVIS records that she used to play and sing along with.

Glory, glory, hallelujah. . . .

Mom picked up her handkerchief, but not because she was sweating. She always got very emotional when something was beautiful.

"The set has fantastic sound too," Dad said. "Not like Ingrid and Gösta's. Theirs sounds tinny."

"Can't you keep quiet?" sighed Mom.

What a terribly long song. . . . The same words over and over.

Out in the kitchen Princess whimpered on and on. But Mom didn't seem to hear her. Ordinarily she would have dashed out to comfort her.

Otherwise everything was just fine now. In the room the candle flames flickered beautifully; the TV was beautiful too with all the stars in the picture. And the florist flowers. And his soft drink.

Why was he feeling in such an odd mood all of a sudden?

Why did he feel a little bit sad?

There they were, sitting, all three so close to each other, Mom's face all smooth, Dad proud of the TV because they had the best set on the market; they were happy and so was he.

And yet the room felt a little bit lonely.

Even though he could reach out and touch both

Mom and Dad—all he had to do was stretch out his hand and he could touch them—they felt so far away. They might be sitting on the moon, with him down here on earth. They were no closer to him than the real ELVIS on TV. It felt like that.

He looked at their hands—Dad's twisting his pipe, Mom's folding her handkerchief in pleats.

Then he looked down at his own hands—it felt lonelier inside his left one, so he placed his right hand over it like a nest. One hand could comfort the other. It's good that a person has two hands, especially at night, when it's winter and dark and cold in the world, and a long way to all the stars. And you're lying in bed.

"What are you doing with your hands?" Mom usually asked. "Healthy children sleep with their hands outside the covers. Like this! One hand on either side."

Why?

When they need each other and they're so much warmer under the covers.

Glory, glory, hallelujah, sang the real ELVIS and his disciples. *Glory, glory, hallelujah. . . .*

CHAPTER

6

Mom wandered around the living room, moving ornaments and playing her ELVIS records.

She'd forgotten to nag him about school because she was thinking about the real ELVIS, whom she'd watched on TV the evening before. Today he could do almost anything he wanted to at home, today she didn't notice anything.

But it turned out to be strangely difficult to find anything to do. It was as if every single idea had stopped when he decided not to go to school. That was probably because he couldn't help thinking about what was happening there, what they were doing, Annarosa and everyone else. But how could he find out without going there?

A kind of nagging had started inside his head, much worse than Mom's. Because when she was insisting that he go to school, then at least he was sure that he wouldn't. She wasn't going to get rid of him that easily; he would show her.

It was strange. And it bothered him. Whenever Mom nagged him, he knew exactly what he wanted. But when she didn't say anything, he wasn't so sure any more. And he didn't want to talk to anyone about it. Grandad and Peter had told him what they thought, he knew their opinions. Grandad said that he could do whatever he wanted, he still had a whole year to go. But Peter thought that he should take a chance and go there again.

"Take another chance!" he said. "You have nothing to lose."

It sounded tempting when Peter said that. "Take a chance" sounded easy and fun. Elvis felt like doing it.

Except for the singing!

They were right, both Peter and Grandad. The question was, which of them was more right? The one who really understood. . . .

All he knew was that Mom was wrong. Even though it looked as if she thought the way Peter did, she really didn't because she was only interested in being left in peace herself. She was only thinking of "putting" him somewhere, but she wasn't going to have her way. No matter how impractical it was, he obviously had to do the opposite of what she was saying. He had to show her!

Otherwise he might not bother about the singing and just take a chance, he really would.

But now since that was impossible . . . ? Well, he'd just have to think of something else. . . .

Couldn't he think up an excuse for going to school—without actually going there? What kind of an excuse?

He needn't necessarily go right inside the building. Inside the schoolyard was good enough.

That was it! Now he had it—

Didn't the schoolyard look unusually cold and desolate? Of course it did! What if he got some flowers to bloom there! They were definitely needed. But it was autumn, no flowers would come up now. He'd just be throwing away seeds. . . .

What about bulbs then? Tulips and hyacinths. They get planted in the autumn. Of course, they wouldn't come up until next year. But they would bloom in the spring, and by then Elvis would have started again, the substitute would be gone, the real teacher would be there, and she wouldn't bother as much about singing; and he would be able to sit wherever he wanted, Annarosa would sit next to him, the sun would shine on his desk top and. . . .

Yes! He'd plant some bulbs! That would be good.

He already had a few that Grandad had given him, in a bag in the cellar. The cellar key—where was it? There, on a hook in the broom closet. Fine. Then the spade. And the watering can. And leave. Quick.

Then he heard Mom's voice:

"Where are you off to, Elvis?"

"Out for a while."

"No sir! No running off now. If you can't go to school, then you can't go outside and run around either."

She caught him at the door.

"What a mess your hair is!" she said. "A real mop. You can't go around looking like that. I'll have to give you a haircut."

She shoved him into the kitchen and got ready to cut his hair. Which was the worst thing that could happen. And he'd thought that she wasn't dangerous today! She turned out to be worse than usual!

She sat him down on a chair with a big cloth over his shoulders. Then she started cutting. He tried to sit still as a mouse, because she said that would make it go much faster. Hair got in his face and tickled him, but he controlled himself. He had to get over to the school with the bulbs before they closed for the day.

The scissors clipped. And snipped.

"Oh dear, why can't I make you have some kind of style?"

Mom grabbed his chin, turned and twisted his head and looked at it critically.

"That's really good," said Elvis.

"No, wait a minute. I'm going to try another kind of cut."

She put on a new ELVIS record and placed the record cover with a picture of the real ELVIS on the kitchen table. Then she took hold of the scissors again.

"I think you should have cute little bangs like his," she said, pointing to his picture with the scissors.

Elvis gave a start. No no, not bangs like that! He wanted his own hair his own way.

"Sit still!" Mom grabbed hold of him. "You can't go out, do you understand, not until I've finished what I want to do."

Then he controlled himself again. He had no choice. But it all boiled and churned inside him and his head was full of small nasty thoughts.

Mom said that he'd be happy that she tried to make him look more stylish. The real ELVIS had such incredibly gorgeous hair.

"Just think, if you looked as nice as he does! Wouldn't it be fun?"

Elvis didn't answer. It was best to keep the small nasty thoughts to himself. But it took a long time to cut ELVIS-bangs, and finally bits of hair got in his eyes, so the whole thing ended in a fight anyway.

He jumped up so violently from the kitchen chair that it crashed over backwards. Mom got angry, of course, but the bangs were finished, she said. She couldn't do much better with his impossible hair, which was nothing but a mess of cowlicks.

Elvis took his watering can and spade.

"I'm going out now," he said.

But!

Of course, he wasn't allowed out. No sir! He didn't deserve that. Not at all.

He didn't understand. She had said that as long as she could do what she wanted to . . . and after all, she got to cut his bangs. . . .

"Maybe, but anyway, I've changed my mind, and there's no point in your nagging. You'll only be sent straight to bed. And you've had fair warning."

He stared at her. She was actually more dangerous today than usual. He saw that from how she acted toward Princess. She hadn't cuddled her at all today.

What had happened? She talked differently too; a little sharp and snappish; almost no discussions. And she hadn't chatted on the phone with her friends either. When they phoned, she told them she was in a hurry, and she didn't call any of them up either.

No—Mom wasn't like herself today.

Elvis put down his spade and the watering can. He sat down on a kitchen chair and thought.

The scissors were still on the kitchen table.

After a while he took the scissors and went into the bathroom and cut off the bangs. It was over in a flash. In no time at all they were gone.

Naturally there was another fight. A worse one than the first, and in fact, he got really fed up with it. Usually Mom got tired first, but not today. He couldn't recognize her. She was bright and sharp and dangerous all day. She said she'd show him who decided things around here.

He wasn't allowed out even for a second, until Dad came home. Dad had forgotten to bring the evening paper, and so Elvis was sent out to buy one, and then he was able to take a quick detour by the cemetery.

He wanted to look at the picture of the Secret. On a day like this he really needed it. And he hadn't been there for a while.

He had a Secret inside him, that is, he could feel it but not see it. Sometimes it was big and all through him, but sometimes it was tiny. Then he scarcely knew where it was and had to be alone to be able to feel it. Because it was still there, all the time. There was no danger of it deserting him, but it could disappear so very, very far inside that he had to search for it.

Like right now. The Secret had shrunk and retreated so deep within him that if he hadn't known for sure it was there, he would have been afraid that he'd lost it.

So he had to go look at the picture.

One time he made a picture of it. He found a black stone on which he painted all the colors in the world. Then he put the stone in a green box. He felt as if he had managed to make a picture of the Secret, and every time he took off the top and held the stone in his hand, he felt the Secret grow and get stronger inside him.

He was the only one who knew about the picture. No one was ever meant to see it. That was why he buried it under the hedge around the cemetery, because no one would think of looking there. But still he was always a bit scared that it would be gone. And now when he didn't find it right away, he felt cold with anxiety. He had to dig in three different places before he found it.

The green box was in quite bad shape. He could see

that he would have to make a new one. But the stone was just as good. He took it in his hand and stood there for a while. He let it slip from one hand to the other—he had to be fair.

The Secret took a little while to start growing, but that didn't matter; he was good at waiting. Now he could feel it, first in his chest, then in his stomach, finally throughout his body.

Then he put the stone back in the box and took out Julia's message that he had found in her house after she moved. He kept it in the box too, because it was very important.

Julia had written:

This is now.

I am me.

Peter is Peter.

And further down on the page he had written himself:

Elvis is Elvis.

He read it and then reread it: *Elvis is Elvis.*

Then he took his pen and added:

Elvis is not ELVIS.

CHAPTER

7

Mom had suddenly stopped talking about school.

Elvis couldn't go there anyway, she said, because of his bangs. The top of his head looked like a field of stubble and he shouldn't let anyone see it.

Too bad he didn't know that in the first place! All he had to do to get out of school was cut off his bangs! How simple!

But Peter and Grandad said that school and bangs didn't have anything to do with each other. He could perfectly well go to school with his stubblehead. They knew that.

But not in his case. In his case what Mom said was what mattered. And she said that he looked too terrible.

That was why she had to talk with the school psychologist. And yes, Elvis went along but he didn't talk and didn't listen.

Afterward Mom told him that the psychologist had decided that he shouldn't go to school.

"So now you've got it all fixed for yourself," said Mom. "You're not *allowed* to go to school! You see, they don't want you there."

So Mom had to put up with him herself. But she said that if he thought it would be a bed of roses, he was wrong. "There'll be some changes here, you'll see. You ought to be ashamed of yourself! But you don't even know enough for that!"

So then Mom said that she had to be ashamed for him. "Imagine having to go to the school psychologist, as if you weren't right in your head. . . . It's mortifying!"

Naturally there were lots of discussions.

Even though Elvis didn't seem upset, in fact he was.

He didn't like all this fuss about the school psychologist. Besides, it wasn't any of her business.

He didn't recall her saying very much when they went there. Mom did most of the talking, he thought.

But then afterward he was told lots of things that she had said. Every day Mom came up with something new, some dumb thing the school psychologist said. So he'd have something to think about!

Grandad just laughed and said that she must have been a real dumbbell. Peter knew several psychologists and he said that they would never say such stupid things, it wasn't possible. Well, Elvis didn't know for sure. . . .

It all seemed very complicated and difficult.

But now anyway he could go out whenever he wanted and, of course, that was good.

But everything about school had got turned around.

Before he *had to go* to school. Now he *wasn't allowed to*.

Naturally it felt rather strange.

That was why he hadn't got anywhere with the bulbs; he hadn't planted them in the schoolyard.

He didn't feel much like meeting anyone just then, not even Annarosa. He wanted to think it all through first—about how first you *had to* and then later you *weren't allowed to do* the very same thing.

But it certainly did look dreary and bare in the schoolyard. Not a single flower. They really did need him there. Actually, going to school had nothing to do with planting flowers, did it?

No, absolutely not.

You have to separate one thing from the other, as Grandad would say. The fact of the matter is, you should.

In that case, he ought to plant the bulbs in the schoolyard!

He didn't have to do it when anyone could see him. For that matter, he'd never planted anything when anyone could watch him. It was more fun that way. Obviously he could do the same thing now.

So Elvis set off in the evening, when twilight was falling, and planted the bulbs in the schoolyard. On his way there he found a few chrysanthemums that were growing much too close together in a public park. He thinned out a couple of them and planted them around in the schoolyard too, so there'd be a few more flowers right away.

No one saw him. The orange flowers against the gray gravel were very pretty. But they looked lonely against the big building. It would be better in the spring, when the bulbs came up.

He wondered whether he'd be going to school then. He really wondered . . . ?

He figured he should go over there sometimes on the sly and water a little in the evening anyway, so that the flowers would do well. He'd like to do that.

But now he had to be on his way.

Granny was sitting in the big room with Mom and Dad when Elvis got home.

They were showing her the color TV. She hadn't seen it yet. Dad switched on all the different knobs and talked about its good features.

"The best set on the market!" he said.

Granny nodded but looked preoccupied. She seemed more interested in Elvis than the TV. But Mom said:

"Granny, did you notice what he did to his hair? Doesn't he look terrible? I can hardly bear to look at him."

Then Granny did something she'd never done before; she gave him a hasty kiss right on his stubblehead and she said that she liked it. Elvis looked at her shyly but he was pleased.

Mom looked at Dad coldly but he was busy fussing with the TV.

"Absolutely first-class," he said. "All the advantages, no drawbacks."

Granny was going to the dentist early the next morning, so she was spending the night with them on the kitchen sofa. She usually went to bed early and wasn't very interested in TV. When they sent Elvis to bed, Granny said that she would go too.

Mom and Dad stayed sitting in front of the TV. They were watching a feature film.

Elvis had nothing against snuggling into bed. He was rather tired.

After a while Granny came to say good night to him. By then he was already in his bed. She stayed and chatted awhile. It was going to be a cold winter, she said, because there were lots of berries on the ash trees.

"How do you know it's because of berries on the ash trees?" asked Elvis.

"That's what they say, but no one knows for sure," Granny answered, "because man proposes and God disposes."

"What if God proposes and man disposes instead?" said Elvis with a little smile.

"Goodness gracious! You shouldn't say that." Granny gestured with both hands. "Where did you pick that up?"

He didn't know. It just came to him.

"Have you said your evening prayer?" asked Granny.

Elvis looked at her blankly. What was that?

"Haven't Mom and Dad taught you to say your evening prayer?"

"Nooo. . . ."

"You poor dear. . . . What a good thing I found out."

Granny pulled up a chair and sat down next to Elvis' bed. She told him to put his hands together and then she'd teach him to say his evening prayer. He could choose the prayer he wanted to learn from three different ones.

Granny clasped her hands together too and recited the prayers for him, one after the other.

"God who holds all children dear. . . ." He'd heard that one before on a kids' TV program. He remembered because he wondered what "holding them deer" meant.

"Does he turn them into deers?" he asked Granny.

"What's that?" said Granny.

"Like deers on leashes?"

But it was *dear* meaning love, not *deer* the animal, and he decided not to choose that prayer.

Then Granny recited one that he hadn't heard:

> "Jesus, tender Shepherd, hear me,
> Bless Thy little lamb tonight;
> Through the darkness be Thou near me,
> Keep me safe till morning light."

Granny recited that one twice. He wanted to be absolutely sure that he heard it properly. He had. No, not that one either.

"I'm no lamb," he said.

"It's just a comparison," said Granny. "People are compared to lambs."

But Elvis shook his head.

"I'm not like a lamb at all."

Granny looked at him very seriously. Then she smiled slightly.

"Not in the least," she agreed.

Then she recited "Our Father." Elvis decided on that one right away, since he couldn't take either of the others. It was a terribly long prayer, even though they just used a bit of it. This much: "Our Father Who art in heaven, hallowed be Thy name. Thy will be done on earth as it is in heaven. Amen."

That would do.

Granny explained a little, and Elvis learned it almost all at once.

That part, "Thy will be done," wasn't so dumb. What would Mom say about him praying to carry out God's will when she always wanted to have her own way!

When Elvis knew the prayer and had finished reciting it, he asked:

"Did Johan recite an evening prayer?"

"Of course he did," said Granny.

"Which one?"

"Different ones. Mostly he recited 'God who holds all children dear.'"

Elvis thought for a while. He listened to sounds from the living room. The feature film was still going on. Okay then. He looked at Granny steadily.

"I know where Johan is," he said.

Granny started a bit, he noticed, then she looked away.

"Do you?" she said quietly.

"Yes, I know."

Both of them stayed quiet for a moment. Granny didn't look at him; she stared straight ahead, right into space.

"I've known it almost all the time," said Elvis, "but I didn't tell anyone, only Grandad."

"Oh, and what did Grandad say?"

"That I was right, that Johan is dead."

"Yes, that's right. Johan is dead," whispered Granny.

Then she gave Elvis a long, steady look.

"I'm very glad that you know," she said.

Elvis nodded, he thought so too. He found out about things—the way they were. He wanted to know.

"But we won't tell Mom that I know. She won't be able to handle it," Elvis whispered to Granny.

"She won't? Why's that?" Granny wondered.

"She only wants me to understand kid stuff, you know. Otherwise there'll be discussions," Elvis explained.

Granny stroked his stubblehead.

"Good night, Elvis," she said. "Thank you for this evening."

"I can recite the evening prayer again if you like," said Elvis, and then he did.

Granny looked happy.

"The movie is probably over now," she whispered. "Sleep well, Elvis."

CHAPTER

8

ORDINARILY ELVIS WOULD almost never look at himself in the mirror, but now he had started doing that to see if the stubble was growing a bit. Dad had evened it somewhat and he really couldn't see that it was quite as ugly as Mom said. In fact, he thought it was better than the bangs that she had made.

But Mom scarcely even wanted to look at him.

Now he remembered that something like this had happened once before, when he was little. He had long, long hair and little curls then.

One day when they were out at Granny and Grandad's, Grandad up and cut off his curls because Elvis was hot and sweaty in the summer heat. And Grandad also thought that Elvis shouldn't go around looking like a girl, because boys all had short hair then.

They were alone at the time, Elvis and Grandad. Elvis agreed with Grandad and he was eager to have his hair cut that time. He didn't put up a fuss at all.

But when Mom saw him, she started a big scene, crying and wailing. And she ran outside.

She didn't want to look at Elvis afterward. She said the same thing now, that Grandad had ruined him. That first time he hadn't known for sure whether his hair would grow back, so he was terribly scared. He thought that he was ruined forever and only fit for the trash.

But his hair grew, though the curls never came back. Mom wouldn't be comforted. She was always examining and touching it. The new hair was different, not the same color. It was coarse and bristly; it used to be much sweeter.

She could never forgive Grandad for that, she said. And since then, she couldn't abide him. She called him "that old man."

"Grandad ruined you for me! You were so cute and sweet."

Elvis listened to this every day and he remembered how it hurt him. He had been "cute and sweet"—without knowing it! That was the first time she said it, then, after his curls had already been cut off. When it was too late! He realized that he'd never be sweet any more. The situation was hopeless now.

Mom didn't act like herself toward him from then on, and he couldn't really expect anything else. He was different and uglier, he wasn't like himself either.

It was Grandad's fault, but Elvis couldn't be angry with him for that. Never! He was exactly the way he had always been when he was with Grandad.

In the end, the whole incident was forgotten. He hadn't thought of it since then, not until right now when he suddenly remembered it all.

It was the same this time, but this time Grandad hadn't ruined him, he did it himself.

He was bigger now and he knew that a person doesn't really change into someone else just because some hair is cut off. But still he felt different—every time Mom said that to him, the words cut into him. And he had to look at himself in the mirror.

He wore his cap when he went out on the street, when people might see him. He was out a lot of the time for he had his own friends, both at the station and over at the messenger service. He also had Peter and Grandad. But now it was autumn, everyone was busy with his own work, and Grandad came into town very seldom. Sometimes Elvis had no one to talk with all day long.

Today looked as if it would be like that. There was a little rain in the air and a cutting wind. He walked and walked; no one was around that he knew.

In fact, it was a typical school day. He walked past the school—the yard was empty. He walked on. After all, he had nothing to do there.

It was going to be a very lonely day. . . .

Of course, there were lots of people in town, rushing about as usual. He felt as if he were the only one who had all the time in the world.

No—there was one other person. An old lady walking in front of him wasn't in a hurry either. She steadied herself with a cane and moved along slowly close to the buildings.

Elvis stayed behind her. He thought of passing her, but then he matched his pace to hers. It might be good for her to have someone walking behind her in case she fell; she looked rather unsteady. Now and then she stopped to rest, and then he stopped too, but she didn't notice him.

Then she stopped in front of a door. She stared hard at it before she opened the door and walked in.

Elvis stood out on the street. What now?

A light drizzle had started to fall. But he didn't feel at all like going home. Instead he walked in the door, following the old lady. If he stayed there awhile, perhaps the drizzle would stop. Strange doors are always interesting.

Inside, he saw the old lady hadn't reached the top of the stairs yet; she was on her way up, at a slow pace, step by step.

Elvis followed her quietly up the stairs—in case she should stumble—but she managed it well. She reached the landing while he was still on the stairs. She didn't turn around once, so she hadn't seen Elvis. Now she stood in front of a door up there looking undecided.

ANTIQUARIAN BOOKSHOP was written on the door. Elvis read the words but didn't know what they meant.

The old lady propped her cane against the wall and fussed with something she had in a big string shopping bag that she was carrying over one arm. Then slowly she pulled a big package out of the bag. She started unwrapping a lot of paper. After quite a bit of trouble and fuss and bother, she was holding a blue book in her hand.

Elvis stared in astonishment.

It was Annarosa's atlas!

The one that wasn't any good in school because the world had changed.

Yes, it was the same one: blue, with a yellow world so the sun could shine on it.

Then this was Annarosa's Old Granny.

What was she going to do with the atlas? Here, on the stairs? She was folding up the paper now and cramming it back into her string bag.

Then she opened the door that said ANTIQUARIAN BOOKSHOP. She had the atlas under one arm and her cane in the other hand and she walked right in.

Without thinking, Elvis dashed straight as an arrow up the stairs and in through the door.

In front of him were rows of bookshelves full of books. There was nothing but books clear up to the ceiling. Down between two of these bookcases walked the old lady with her atlas.

Elvis tiptoed after her.

They walked as though through a maze. There were bookcases set up on the floor with passages between them. What if they could never find their way out! They walked and walked.

Suddenly an old man stood at the end of one of the paths between the books. He came toward them. The old lady met him, but Elvis stood a little way off. The old man must have thought that Elvis was with the old lady because he didn't bother about Elvis.

"What can I do for you?" he asked the old lady.

She handed him the atlas.

"What can I get for this?" she asked.

The old man took it and leafed through it a little, but then he gave it right back to her.

"We're deluged with old atlases like that," he said. "Unfortunately we have no use for it."

But the old lady wouldn't take back the book. She looked insulted.

"I've had it all my life," she said. "It's old."

"I'm sure it has more value to you than to us," answered the old man. "Maps have to be really very old to have any interest."

The old lady pointed her finger at him.

"Look at me!" she said, her finger trembling slightly. "Aren't I old? The atlas is almost as old as I am."

But the old man only shook his head.

"Perhaps," he said, "but for us it's not old enough. I'm sorry, but that's the way it is."

He still tried to hand the atlas back to her. She wouldn't accept it. She took a long time to get out what she wanted to say.

"Not old enough! Well, I'm the best judge of that. . . ."

The old man looked bewildered.

"I could give you fifty cents for it," he said.

But then the old lady grabbed the atlas away from him. She hugged it to her with unexpected strength.

"Oh no! I don't intend to be taken for a ride! This is a treasure, I tell you."

She trembled again and turned her back on the old man, who was completely dazed and confused. She walked right past Elvis without noticing him.

"Oh no!" she said again. "Oh no!"

Elvis also turned his back on the old man and followed her.

They disappeared again between the bookcases; she walked first and he followed her. They walked and walked. How would they find their way out? She breathed heavily with every step. He heard each breath, and when she stopped, he did too, but she didn't see him.

They were probably lost, but all they could do was go on. They'd surely find some exit or other. It was quite exciting—if only he could stop worrying about the old lady. She was going to die, Annarosa said so. . . .

What if she fell down dead right in front of him!

She stopped more and more often.

"Oh no!" she said each time. "Oh no!"

New paths between bookcases opened up all the time with new walls of books. A strange idea, to build walls out of books!

After an eternity, finally a door appeared saying EXIT.

The old lady disappeared through it and Elvis followed her.

But it wasn't the door they'd used to come in. It was completely different stairs. The old lady wasn't disturbed by this at all. She wrapped the paper around the atlas again, and Elvis walked past her without her noticing him.

"Imagine!" she said. "Trying to cheat an old person. What times we're living in!"

She was talking to herself, not to Elvis. She was very upset.

Elvis understood. He thought that she had been badly treated too.

But the atlas was saved!

She started down the stairs again. The atlas was in her string bag. She looked carefully at every step she took and put her feet down carefully. It took a long time, but Elvis certainly had all the time in the world. . . .

Finally they were all the way down. First she went out through the door, then he followed her.

They came out onto a completely different street, not the one they'd been on before. Elvis hardly knew his way around. But it didn't matter. He had definitely decided to follow the old lady all the way home. Mostly for his own sake.

Then he'd know where Annarosa lived.

He shouldn't miss this opportunity.

Their slow wandering began again, up one street and down another.

It was hard to know whether Annarosa lived far away or not. All roads seem longer when you walk very slowly like that. On the other hand, he had plenty of time to memorize the way properly.

In case he wanted to go there several times. . . .

Because he didn't think that he'd say hello to Annarosa now. He just wanted to find out where she lived, so he'd know.

You shouldn't do everything all at once, you should have something left to do—and to think about too. . . .

At last they arrived. The old lady slowly disappeared into a courtyard. She went around the corner of a house and he didn't see her any more. Elvis waited awhile in case he might see her in one of the windows, but she didn't show up. It was hard to see in; there were lots of flowers in all the windows. In a couple of windows there were big bouquets in tall vases, not potted plants.

The house Annarosa lived in was green. The roof was black. It had two floors, and he really wanted to know which floor she lived on.

There were four windows on the ground floor and four above. He really wished he knew which one was Annarosa's.

Between the windows there were round bushes with white berries.

He crept over and took a berry from each bush.

The gables had windows too but no bushes.

He would have liked to look around the courtyard but he didn't do that.

Maybe another time.

He should go home now.

It had started raining hard. He would be sopping wet by the time he got home.

It didn't matter.

He had found Annarosa's house.

CHAPTER

9

ELVIS HAD BEEN outside Annarosa's house twice. Both times he walked over there in the evening because it was easier to see who was moving around inside when the lights were on.

The first time no one appeared, even though all the windows were lit except ones on the ground floor.

He went into the yard and carefully opened the door to the lobby but didn't dare step inside. He stood in the doorway listening. Not a sound anywhere, as if no one were home even though all the lights were on.

When he came out onto the street again, he thought that the curtain in the one dark room moved a bit, it definitely did, but he didn't see anyone there or anywhere else, so he had to leave with his mission unaccomplished.

The second time was just the opposite: all the lights were off in the house, except for the window where the curtain had moved the day before. Now there was a light on in there. A ceiling light. Also a couple of candles flickered here and there on the ground floor. Clearly no one was home upstairs. But down below, the place was full of people. People moved about in their rooms; it looked as if they were dancing. The only place no one could be seen was in the room with the light on.

Elvis tried to pick out people who were moving around, but it was difficult in the dark. There seemed to be nothing but adults, no children.

So that meant no Annarosa.

That meant she lived upstairs, where no one was home.

But just as he was about to leave, he caught sight of her. For a brief second he glimpsed her in the window where the ceiling light was on. There she was!

He was sure even though he only saw her briefly so far away. He could tell because of her two little tufts of hair. She always wore her hair that way.

Then he knew that she lived on the ground floor.

The next day he went over around noon, when she should be in school. He brought a bulb to plant under the window where he'd seen her the day before.

A surprise bulb: he had no idea what kind of flower was hidden inside it. That was why he chose it. It wouldn't be right to choose any one kind of flower for Annarosa. Perhaps he could have picked out the right seed—but not a bulb. Bulbs are more fun when you don't have any idea what they are.

No one in sight, so he could plant the bulb in peace and quiet. He had his watering can, and afterward he watered it properly.

While he was standing there sprinkling the water evenly over the earth, the window opened and Annarosa peered out.

"Hello! What are you doing?" she asked.

"Planting a bulb," Elvis answered, giving the bulb a final sprinkle.

"A bulb?" said Annarosa. "The kind we put in a lamp?"

Right, people do put bulbs in lamps, but this was the kind you plant so flowers will grow, Elvis explained. "Like onions, they're bulbs too."

Annarosa asked him to wait a minute. She came right out with a bag of onions from her kitchen. They were big and fine, and there were plenty to put one under each window. There was even an onion left over.

"Then we'll put one more bulb under your window," said Elvis.

But Annarosa had no window of her own, she shared a room with her mom and her granny. The window Elvis thought was hers was really Old Granny's, that is, Old Granny had her own room, because she wanted to be by herself.

"But you can plant it there anyway," she said. "It doesn't matter."

But Elvis hesitated. Maybe it wasn't necessary, since Annarosa had said that Old Granny was going to die soon, and then she'd get to see masses of flowers.

"Oh no, that's just what she says. She's terribly old and she'll never die," said Annarosa. "She'll get to be ever so old."

Oh well, in that case, he had nothing against her having the bulb under her window.

When they had finished planting, Annarosa said:

"You can come in with me as long as we don't wake Mommy."

Her mother worked at night so she had to sleep in the daytime. Elvis promised not to wake her.

"Do we dare talk?" he asked when they were in the hall.

"Sure, if we whisper," said Annarosa. She pointed to the door of the room where her mother was sleeping, and put her finger to her lips.

Then she showed him their living room, where her mother had her parties. A whole lot of glasses and coffee cups and ashtrays were still scattered around from the last party.

Old Granny's door was ajar, but they went straight into the kitchen. It was no use bothering Old Granny. She had a great deal to think over that happened long ago, so much that she couldn't keep up with what was happening now. Her head had got all filled up long ago, she couldn't fit any more into it, Annarosa explained to Elvis. Then she closed the kitchen door carefully behind them.

It was a big kitchen, rather like his at home, but not as tidy. There were dishes everywhere, and shoes and newspapers and paper bags with trash on the floor. Elvis thought how his mom would have a fit if she saw it.

Annarosa stood in the middle of the room looking around.

"There's not much to do here," she said. "All my things are in the bedroom. We had people over last night and Granny hasn't got around to the washing up."

She opened the refrigerator door.

"What would you like?" she asked Elvis.

He looked at her, startled. Was she really allowed to get things out of the refrigerator? He never could. If he wanted something, he always had to ask for it first. Otherwise he was stealing, Mom would say.

But not in Annarosa's home. She could take anything she wanted. Her mom worked in a restaurant and her granny in a supermarket. They always brought so much food home every day that it was good to eat it up. And today they had an extra amount because of the guests last night.

"Not the shrimps," Elvis said. "We can't take them, can we?"

In the middle of the refrigerator there was a big blue bowl of pink shrimps.

Yes, sure. Annarosa immediately took the shrimps out and cleared a place for them on the kitchen table.

Then she got glasses and soft drinks too. Then she showed him how to peel shrimps.

"But what if your mom wants them when she wakes up!" whispered Elvis. He didn't understand how Annarosa dared do this.

But she took it all lightly. She said that her mom

could get more at the restaurant in the evening any-way. They knew the man who owned the place.

"I do too," she whispered. "Maybe he is my dad, you know."

Elvis pulled the head off one of the shrimps the way she had taught him.

"Does he play soccer?" he asked.

She didn't know. She didn't know him too well, be-cause she wasn't absolutely sure that he was her dad. There were several to choose from.

"But Mom is rather tired of all that now," she said. "You get that way in the long run."

Elvis nodded. He wasn't really keeping up with the conversation, but everything she was saying sounded right and obvious, so all he had to do was agree.

He looked at her. She was different at home than she was in school, though her eyes were the same. But when she talked, she seemed different. In school she was quite quiet, never said very much. But maybe she was chatting a lot now because they had to whisper. People always have more to say when they whisper.

"Do you like whispering like this?" he asked.

"I'm used to it," she answered, whispering on about all sorts of things.

Elvis peeled shrimps and ate them and drank his soft drink and listened.

She told about the party they had the evening be-fore. They danced almost all night long. That was why she stayed home from school today. They slept late this morning.

"Anyway, why have you been away from school so long yourself?" she asked. "Have you been ill all this time?"

Elvis didn't feel like talking about it, so he asked about the atlas instead, but he didn't tell her that he had run into Old Granny.

"Do you still have the atlas?" he asked.

Yes indeed. It was in Old Granny's room. And now she'd found out how valuable it was. Everyone tried to steal it from her. Annarosa couldn't take it to school with her any more. But she'd get it when Old Granny died. So it wouldn't be hers for a long time.

"Aren't you allowed to look at it?" asked Elvis.

Oh yes, as much as she wanted.

Well, that was the main thing. Elvis looked at her and gave a little smile. Here he was sitting next to her, with a blue bowl full of pink shrimps and the atlas within reach. It was unbelievable but true. Everything else felt unimportant.

"You didn't hear what I asked," said Annarosa suddenly.

"What?"

"Why aren't you in school? Since you're not ill?"

"I quit," Elvis answered.

"You're not allowed to! Everyone has to go to school."

But Elvis shook his head. Yes, true—everyone who is allowed to has to go.

"But some people aren't allowed to."

She looked at him doubtfully. "Who isn't allowed to?"

Elvis took off his cap that he'd been wearing all the time.

"People who cut off all their hair and don't look like everyone else," he whispered, pointing to his stubblehead.

Annarosa still looked as though she doubted him. She didn't take him seriously until he told her what the school psychologist said to Mom.

"You shouldn't have cut off your hair," she said. "I want you to go to school."

"Me too," whispered Elvis, and now he really felt what a misfortune it was.

They exchanged a puzzled look. Annarosa pushed the blue bowl toward him.

"Have another shrimp," she said comfortingly.

They each took a shrimp and peeled them quietly. Then Elvis put his cap back on. He was heartbroken.

Annarosa shoved the bowl toward him again.

"Take another," she said.

He did. She did too.

"That'll make you feel better anyway," she said.

"Yes," said Elvis.

Then she had an idea.

"Can't you get a wig?" she asked. "Lots of people wear them these days."

But he didn't think so. Wigs were expensive. He knew that because there'd been a discussion at home about Mom getting one so she wouldn't have to go to the hairdresser so often. But she couldn't afford it.

Then Annarosa remembered that her mommy had a hairpiece somewhere.

"You're welcome to borrow it," she said, "because Mom has changed her hair color, so she doesn't need it any more."

Her mom's hair was red now and the hairpiece was brown. Annarosa took off Elvis' cap and studied the color of his hair. The hairpiece might be a bit darker, but that was nothing to worry about. She had tried it on herself once. She and Elvis had almost the same color hair, and on her it looked fine.

She'd hunt for the hairpiece that evening after Mom left for the restaurant. She promised not to give up until she found it, so that Elvis could start going to school again. It was very important, she said, looking at him with her eyes wide open.

"Yes," whispered Elvis. He couldn't imagine why he hadn't realized before quite how important it was. He did think this whole business about the hairpiece sounded a bit strange, but what else could he do . . . ?

"Necessity knows no laws," whispered Annarosa.

That's what her Old Granny said, which meant that you just have to! Even if maybe you don't want to.

"I want to," whispered Elvis.

Okay then. If he came back in the evening, after Mom left, then Annarosa could try the hairpiece on him. Mom left around six o'clock. She might as well not know they were borrowing it.

"But she'll get it back," said Annarosa, "as soon as your stubblehead grows out. She's forgotten about it. And she has red hair now anyway."

Elvis promised to come back at six o'clock.

"Perhaps you can look at the atlas too," whispered Annarosa comfortingly. "You'll see, everything will work out."

CHAPTER

10

As soon as Elvis got home, he asked Mom what time it was. And then he went on asking the same question over and over. Because he had to be back at Annarosa's house at six o'clock. He had to keep track of the time.

Finally he was driving Mom really crazy.

"I can't keep looking at the clock every minute! Stop nagging me! I've already got a headache. . . ."

Then the phone rang and Mom stayed on it chatting.

Elvis trudged back and forth looking at the kitchen clock. It ticked and ticked, but from what he could see, it wasn't moving. But if he went away for a moment, the hands moved immediately. It was very irritating. And anxious-making too. He couldn't bear it any longer.

He just had to learn how to tell time, obviously.

So he set off to see Peter.

As luck would have it, Peter was home. He'd just had a wisdom tooth pulled and it was hurting him. He was sitting there, uncomfortable and bored.

"So then can't you teach me how to tell time?" Elvis asked.

Peter had nothing against the idea. He got out an old battered alarm clock and started the lesson.

It wasn't difficult at all. Much easier than learning to ride a bike or swim. And easier than learning to read too. How dumb of him not to have learned about time before. Now he wouldn't have to always nag Mom and give her a headache.

He didn't have to worry about being too late either, because he found out that he had plenty of time. He even had time to help Peter fix the alarm clock. That was harder, but in the end they got it going.

Then Peter gave Elvis the clock. He had another and he said he didn't need it. It was big and ticked very loudly and jumped when the alarm rang. Elvis thought it was sad for Peter to give away such a nice clock, but Peter said that Elvis should have it by way of thanks because now he was rid of the toothache and he thought it was because of Elvis.

"I'm so glad you came and gave me something else to think about," said Peter.

That made Elvis smile.

"You get rid of your toothache because of me, but all I do to Mom is give her a headache," he said. "Funny, isn't it?"

Yes, mysterious. They both had to laugh at that. Peter didn't understand it either, but it wasn't worth fussing about.

Elvis didn't think so either.

When he got back home, Dad had come from work.

Dad was in an unusually good mood. Elvis showed him the alarm clock and explained that now they could ask him the time, because now he knew.

Dad asked and Elvis answered. Correctly every time. Mom asked too, and they thought that he was clever.

"Oh, so that's why you kept running in and asking what time it was. If you'd asked me, I could have taught you," Mom said.

It sounded as if she were a little sorry about it.

Though that wasn't why he had asked her the time; he just didn't want to arrive late at Annarosa's. But Elvis didn't say anything. He let her think that. Let her have some regrets: there was so much she never regretted at all. In fact, he didn't pity her that much. Especially when she said that the alarm clock Peter had given him was junk. She said it was old-fashioned and fit for the trash and he wasn't to keep it where it could be seen because it wasn't decorative. But Dad didn't agree, he said the important thing was that it worked.

"Those old clocks usually have very sound workings," he said.

"I don't want that old thing around messing up the house," Mom said.

She was never sorry when she said things like that. Besides, Elvis didn't intend to leave the clock around. Of course, he'd keep it with him—always—so he'd know what time it was. It fitted in his jacket pocket. So Mom didn't have to be concerned about it.

You could tell that Dad was in a very good mood. At suppertime he picked up the evening paper and started chuckling. He turned to one page and said to Mom:

"Here, listen to this! Just listen!"

Then he started reading aloud. They had written about the real ELVIS in the paper.

It said that he was pasty and potbellied. And that he couldn't sing. All he could do was slur his words and howl and talk through his nose. And leer unpleasantly, it said. And kick. And shake his knees. And sweat. And kiss girls.

Dad could hardly read, he was laughing so hard.

Mom got angry and tried to take the paper away from him. But Dad stood up and went on reading. It said that the real ELVIS was repulsive too. And worthless. And hung over. And fat.

Now Mom tried to get the paper and gash it so that it ripped to pieces. Dad just laughed. Then she began to cry.

Elvis sat on his chair and stirred his raspberry cream.

All kinds of things were in the papers.

He didn't know . . .

What to think . . .

Or believe . . .

If this were true. . . .

He stirred and stirred his dessert.

Plainly—the real ELVIS did sweat and kiss girls; Elvis had seen that for himself. But potbellied? He didn't think so anyway. And pasty? No—he wasn't especially pale. . . .

Mom just cried. She sobbed that Dad was nasty.

"Nasty! I just thought you'd be interested," snickered Dad.

Mom didn't answer. She sat down and Dad took the paper again.

Elvis asked, "Does it really say that he can't sing?"

Yes, it did. Dad read it aloud one more time. Elvis listened solemnly. This was important to him, not because he could judge at all, but because he *wanted* it to be true that the real ELVIS could sing. He had thought before that he *didn't* want it. But now suddenly he felt just the opposite. The real ELVIS *had* to be good at singing. Otherwise everything would be so dumb. Nothing should be that dumb.

Then he wouldn't know what to believe.

All his life he had heard ELVIS records. Mom played them almost every day.

He stirred the dessert. How difficult and confusing everything was.

And now they were arguing again. . . .

Mom said that he could sing!

Dad said that he'd never been able to sing.

Now they both stood up. Facing each other. Stiff as boards.

Mom wasn't crying any more.

Dad wasn't laughing.

They just stared. Angrily.

Mom tried to grab the paper.

Dad hit her with it on the arm.

Then she caught the paper and tore it to shreds. She tore and tore it.

Dad got really angry. He hadn't read the sports pages yet.

Mom started blubbering again.

Dad repeated what was in the paper, but he wasn't laughing.

"Potbellied! Pasty-faced!" he said.

"Potbellied yourself," said Mom.

"Says you!" answered Dad.

Elvis was about to see if he had a potbelly too when he knocked his plate and spilled raspberry cream all over himself.

Mom shrieked and covered her face.

"Clumsy slob," said Dad.

So Elvis never did get over to Annarosa's home that evening, even though now he knew how to tell time and could be punctual. Nobody cared about that now.

Right after supper he was sent straight to bed.

CHAPTER

11

WHEN ELVIS ARRIVED at Annarosa's the next evening, both her mom and granny were at home. Old Granny too, of course.

Mom opened the door for him. She had very red hair.

Annarosa was sitting in the kitchen, writing a whole line of Fs. Then she was supposed to write a whole line of Gs too. She tore a page out of her notebook so that Elvis could do the lesson too. Because he would be going to school the next morning. She wanted him to, she said.

"I couldn't make it yesterday, you see," said Elvis.

"I knew that," she said.

Elvis did the lesson too. He knew it already but he wrote it anyway for good measure.

Annarosa's mom had the evening off. But the hairpiece was all ready. It wasn't easy to find; Annarosa had spent almost the whole evening looking for it. She quickly pulled out a tuft of brown hair from her pocket and showed him.

"Later, when they watch TV, we can go into the bathroom and try it," she whispered. "Then I'll show you how to put it on."

Annarosa's granny came out into the kitchen and lay down on the kitchen sofa. She put a big pillow under her legs, so she could keep her feet up off the floor.

"You get terrible pains when you have to stand on your feet all day," she said.

She was quite fat; she lay there looking at Elvis.

"Are you in the same class?" she asked.

Yes, they were. Annarosa hurried to answer so that Elvis wouldn't be able to say that he had stopped going. He saw that she didn't want him to say that. Then Granny talked about school, Annarosa answered and Elvis agreed.

"It's a real pleasure to meet one of your little school friends, Annarosa," Granny said. "We haven't seen any of them here at home before. We were almost wondering whether you had any friends at all."

Then Annarosa blushed a little; Elvis noticed and knew exactly why. Granny was talking about things that were none of her business. Typical grown-up talk that happens when grown-ups are around. He knew that so well. But he also noticed that it was worse when it was your own family, not someone else's. He wouldn't have realized this if he hadn't felt the same thing before, and if Annarosa hadn't blushed.

"Don't you want anything?" Granny asked.

"I'm not hungry," answered Annarosa.

"Not you. Perhaps Elvis is."

"He had shrimps yesterday. Don't you want to watch TV?"

Granny laughed but stayed right where she was.

"So you want to get rid of me?" she said. "The program doesn't begin for another fifteen minutes, so you'll have to put up with me for a while longer."

Then she asked Elvis if he still wasn't hungry after the shrimps he'd had yesterday. He didn't know how he was supposed to answer that, so he didn't say anything one way or the other.

"You'll find some delicious little meatballs in the refrigerator, if you'd like them," she said. "All you have to do is get them. Go ahead!"

But Elvis didn't want them. Then Annarosa's mom came into the kitchen and got out the meatballs. She took some herself and then offered the platter to Elvis without a word. Annarosa didn't want any, but Elvis took some.

Mom talked the whole time with Granny about someone at the restaurant who was really sloppy. Now and then she offered Elvis the meatballs without looking at him. She didn't ask him anything and hardly looked at him. It was really great—as if it was the most natural thing in the world that he was sitting right there, nothing to get all excited about.

Then she dumped a deck of cards on the kitchen table and asked Granny if she felt up to playing a game. But then they remembered the TV program and both of them hurried off into the living room.

Annarosa took the hairpiece out of her pocket again.

They went into the bathroom.

Elvis asked whether Old Granny was going to watch TV too. He saw that her door was still ajar but he couldn't see her in there.

"She has her own TV in her head," said Annarosa, "and she says it's more fun, so she never watches TV."

"What about the atlas?" Elvis wondered. "When are we going to look at that?"

Not now anyway. Annarosa was combing the hairpiece.

"Isn't it neat?" she asked.

Elvis looked at it timidly. It sure was fine, but he felt quite hesitant anyway, he couldn't help it. Was he really going to wear that?

"It's just so you can start school again," said Annarosa. "Only for that."

She put down the seat top on the toilet. Elvis was to sit there while she tried it on him.

He did as she said—but if it had been anyone else,

he felt sure he would never have gone along with this.

She handed him a dish of hairpins; he was to hand them to her one by one. Then she started fussing on the top of his head. She fiddled and worked hard; it took a lot of hairpins.

"This is a hellish job," she said.

He was aware of it. She had to use rubber bands too, because the stubble was really too short to fasten anything to it, which meant she had to comb some hair from the back of his head forward, and that was better. But to make it really stay in place, she had to use some tape too.

There! Finally it was finished. The hairpiece was a trifle long, compared with his own, so she had to trim a bit off, but she didn't dare cut very much. Anyway it was fine, she said. And the color wasn't too terribly dark.

"Now you can look at yourself in the mirror!"

Elvis climbed up on the toilet seat and looked.

He wasn't much of a judge of such things, but he did think that he had a terrible lot of hair now.

"Lots of hair is nice," said Annarosa.

"Yes, sure, but . . . ?"

"And you can't see the stubble at all. Not a trace!"

"No, you really can't. . . ."

"Well, that's the point."

"Yes, but still. . . ."

"Isn't this what the school psychologist wanted?"

Yes it was. Exactly. Mom had said that the school psychologist wanted his hair to grow back.

"Well, now she can't say a thing."

"No, she certainly can't, but still. . . ."

"Okay then! You're all set."

Yes, of course. Since that was the way it was. But Elvis thought that the school psychologist really shouldn't have anything to do with his hair at all.

No, she shouldn't, Annarosa agreed. But now that the school psychologist had got herself mixed up in it, what else could he do? He had to defend himself, didn't he?

Sure, of course you have to, somehow, but. . . .

"So you had to have a hairpiece!" said Annarosa with determination, and Elvis didn't protest, because she was obviously right.

She was standing on the toilet seat beside him. She was gazing at her handiwork in the mirror, looking satisfied.

"It's not too bad at all," she said. "If you can do as good a job yourself. You have to allow plenty of time."

Then she told him to pay attention while she showed him how to put the hairpiece on before he went to school early the next morning.

Elvis was a bit shaken. He hadn't figured on fixing the hairpiece by himself the next morning.

"I'll never be able to stick it on," he said.

"You just have to," she said. There was nothing to it

as long as he listened carefully. He could take the tape
and hairpins and everything else he'd need. It would
all work out perfectly!

"But what if Mom sees me!"

Annarosa wouldn't hear any objections. Of course,
he had to lock himself in the bathroom and wear his
cap. He wore it most of the time anyway, so his mom
wouldn't think much about it. Later when he got to
school, Annarosa could help him fix the hairpiece if
necessary.

She was so eager and so determined that all he could
do was go along with her. Elvis really made a great
effort to understand when she showed him what to do
with the hairpiece. Then they took it off. But the tape
was hard to remove.

"That can stay on till tomorrow," said Annarosa.
"It's just as well, then you won't have to put on any
more."

But Mom looked Elvis over from top to toe every
evening before he went to bed. She'd really pounce on
him if he tried to creep into bed with lots of tape in
his hair. So he didn't dare leave it there.

Annarosa said that she could walk around with her
whole head covered with tape and no one would notice except possibly Old Granny, and she'd only ask:

"Is that something newfangled?"

Everything she didn't understand or thought was
peculiar she just assumed was a new fad, something she

had to put up with. That meant Annarosa had quite an easy time at home. She could do what she wanted most of the time.

At last they got off all the tape. Some of his hair came off with it too, but it didn't hurt so he didn't mind.

Annarosa shoved the hairpiece and all the combs and pins and tape into a paper bag.

But now it was too late to go into Old Granny's room and look at the atlas; that would have to wait for another time.

"Besides, only schoolchildren can look at it," said Annarosa. "So you'd better start school again tomorrow! Otherwise you'll never be able to look at the atlas."

That was why she didn't want to let on that Elvis had quit school, she explained, when Granny was there, because then Old Granny might have gathered that. Annarosa couldn't look at the atlas herself until she started going to school.

"So now you understand!" she said solemnly.

Yes indeed—Elvis understood.

He was going to start school the next morning.

CHAPTER

12

IT WAS A LUCKY THING that Mom was so sleepy every morning and that Dad had to leave so early. That way Elvis had a whole hour to himself to arrange the hairpiece. You couldn't see his stubble at all. That was good.

But otherwise what he saw in the mirror wasn't the world's tidiest hairdo.

It would look slightly better with his cap on.

Mom slept like a log. Sometimes he was lucky—she didn't even hear him when he rooted around in the hall closet for his school things. Or when he opened the outer door and set off. So for once he got away without her hollering out the window after him.

He wasn't so worried about what was going to happen. The nearer he got to school, the more certain he became that what he was doing was right.

No matter what they all said, Mom or the teacher or

the school psychologist, sooner or later—with or without the hairpiece—he would have to take another chance. He knew that as soon as Peter said it, and in fact, it was dumb of him to have waited so long.

Now that he was on his way, nothing would stop him. When he saw the school building, he took out his alarm clock and looked at it. Luckily he was early. Annarosa would have time to fix the hairpiece.

After he got inside the school gates, he looked but couldn't find her anywhere. The schoolyard was already full of kids. She should have been there by then to have time to help him.

She couldn't be thinking of coming there late!

He found a place where he could see everyone who passed through the gates. He looked in the direction that she would be coming from, but she was nowhere to be seen down the whole length of the long street.

He waited and waited. He wasn't worried but maybe a bit disappointed. Yesterday she'd been so eager for him to come.

The bell rang and everyone walked toward the school door.

Annarosa hadn't come. It had never occurred to him that she might not show up. What should he do now? Should he wait for her and be late with her? Because surely she was on her way?

He watched the last pupils disappear through the door. Strangely enough, this didn't worry him either.

He never worried when he really set his mind on something. Now he knew for sure what he wanted—though all the others always wanted something different. That was what made it all so difficult.

That was why there would be such a big fuss.

He took out his alarm clock and compared it with the school clock. They said exactly the same time. He couldn't wait any longer.

So here he was at the school gates.

He had already walked through them.

But over there was the door to the school.

He had to go through that too.

Between the gates and the door was the yard, big and empty and desolate. He had to cross that first. All alone.

Because Annarosa wasn't coming. He knew that now. The others had already gone inside and she wasn't coming.

So then he had to go in all alone, he thought. And he did just that! He walked calmly across the yard up to the door, opened it and walked right in.

He found the classroom right away; not everyone had gone in yet, so he wasn't too late. At that very moment, Miss Magnusson appeared. From the other direction. They met.

"You're here, Elvis!" she said, but didn't look surprised.

Elvis nodded. She hurried the others on. They went

quickly into the classroom, all of them, so Miss Magnusson and Elvis were left alone out in the hall.

"Weren't you going to stop school?" she said.

"Yes, but I'm taking another chance," Elvis answered, starting to unbutton his jacket.

"Are you?" said Miss Magnusson. "Really?"

"Yes, I might as well," said Elvis.

"And how many days are in a chance? Or is it only for today?" she asked.

Elvis hadn't decided, so he didn't know.

"Well, you'll have to decide," said Miss Magnusson. "You can have this one day, but after school today I'd like to know what you've decided."

Elvis promised to think about it during the day and give her an answer.

Suddenly Miss Magnusson said, "What's that ticking?"

Oh, the alarm clock. Elvis took it out of his pocket and put it in his schoolbag instead, so he could take it with him into the classroom.

"Are you taking it along in case you might fall asleep during class?" Miss Magnusson asked, laughing.

It was a happy laugh, so Elvis laughed too.

Then she said, "Now do let's join the others. But aren't you going to take off your cap?"

Naturally. Elvis ripped off his cap without thinking. The cap that he had planned on taking off very carefully! He forgot! So the hairpiece came off with the cap.

A heavy shower of hairpins fell all around him.

And there he was in front of Miss Magnusson with his stubblehead and a lot of tape and clips and rubber bands everywhere. And the hairpiece curling out of his cap. It looked as if he were holding a serpent's nest in his hand.

At first Miss Magnusson didn't know what to think.

Was he poking fun at her?

What was he trying to do?

She decided not to say a word, and let him clear it up. It wasn't easy for her to figure what to say anyway.

She tried not to look dismayed or about to scold or about to laugh; she looked at him steadily. The longer she looked, the surer she was that he wasn't playing a game with her at all.

So Elvis only met a friendly, interested look in Miss Magnusson's eyes.

His stubble was exposed. There was no point trying to hide it any more. School was over for him now. He'd better turn right around before the discussion started, because discussions were the worst things he knew, and he had enough of them at home. But she still hadn't said anything.

He looked at her. She looked back. Right into his eyes. She didn't look at his stubble at all. Well, hadn't she noticed it? She must have! Besides, the school psychologist must have told on him.

Shouldn't he say something before he left? Shouldn't he explain this business about the hairpiece? He pointed to the hairpiece.

"I cut my hair a bit, you see, up here," he said, pointing.

Miss Magnusson looked at the stubble. Then she looked at the curls in his cap.

"Did you think it looked too short?" she asked.

Couldn't she see that it was?

She pointed to the hairpiece. "Is that why you fixed yourself up with that?"

"Yes, because that's what the school psychologist said, you see."

"Did the school psychologist say you should have false hair?" Miss Magnusson asked, and now she did look both a bit confused and ready to laugh. But that was fair enough in the circumstances; Elvis felt the same. The psychologist shouldn't meddle in things like this. Miss Magnusson sounded as if she thought so too, so then Elvis explained to her how it all happened.

No, the hairpiece wasn't something the psychologist had thought up. He didn't mean that. He'd borrowed it so no one could see his stubble. Because Mom said that the psychologist said that he wasn't allowed to go to school until he looked like everyone else again. He looked too dumb and silly now and no one wanted to see him. That's how it was.

"But there's no rule about short hair in school," said Miss Magnusson. "There must have been a misunderstanding." She didn't think that the hairpiece made it better.

"What a lot of trouble you went to!" she said, looking at all the tape on his head. She would help him get it off.

"I'll just go tell the class what to do meanwhile. Wait a minute!"

She went into the classroom and told the others to read awhile, that she would be back soon. Then she helped Elvis with the tape and gave him some paper to wrap the hairpiece in.

"The class doesn't have to see it," she said, putting

it way in the bottom of Elvis' schoolbag. "Because I have a feeling that whoever lent it to you would rather like to get it back all in one piece."

She combed his hair a little and told him that if he hadn't said anything, she wouldn't have noticed the stubble. She didn't think that anyone else would pay any attention to it either. As long as he didn't bring it up himself.

"Mom will," said Elvis. "She thinks about it all the time, as soon as she sees me."

"Of course. Mothers always notice more than anyone else," said Miss Magnusson. "They have to, of course."

She thought that in school no one paid much attention to things like that as long as you don't go around making a fool of yourself. But Elvis wouldn't do that.

Miss Magnusson was right. No one noticed his hair when they went into the classroom. No one said anything during recess either. He was left in peace.

A girl from another class came up and asked him what his name was. But before he answered, he asked her what her name was.

Her name was Britt. Then he said that his name was Elvis Karlsson, but she didn't believe him. And then two others from his class came over and said that was really true.

She still looked disbelieving.

She asked, "Why are you called *Elvis*?"

He told her the truth, that he was named after the real ELVIS.

Then her eyes got a strange and quite dangerous look in them.

"The *real* Elvis," she repeated, staring at him. "That means you're the *false* Elvis?"

He was really taken aback by this idea, because he had never thought of it. Then he burst out laughing. The others looked at him piercingly and not quite trustfully, but he didn't notice.

"False Elvis . . . Felvis," he said, laughing.

The others laughed too. Britt as well.

"Felvis!" they repeated. "Felvis!"

Then Elvis thought of, "Pelvis. No . . . Helvis!"

He didn't know where he got it all from and it made him all the more delighted. It was fun to think up names.

The others caught his mood and jumped around him, trying to think up more names too.

A girl who was twice as tall as he came over and whirled him around.

"Hi, Kelvis!" she said.

The others whooped with joy. There was nothing dangerous in Britt's eyes any more, only laughter. She went spinning around with Elvis too and pulled his cap all the way down to the tip of his nose, but as a joke, while all the others shouted:

"Kelvis! Best there is!"

Elvis was hot all over. He'd never felt like this before, not with kids, only with Peter. He stretched his arms straight out from his body. They started cranking his arms as if he were a helicopter getting ready to take off. Straight into the sky. That was just how he felt—as if flying would be a cinch.

"Hey, listen! This guy's ticking!" someone shouted.

They all stopped and listened and stared with their mouths open. They looked as if they seriously believed that he had a motor inside and was about to rise up into the air any second now. They looked so surprised.

"It's just my alarm clock," said Elvis, and he showed it to them.

No one had a clock like his! They looked at it respectfully. The girl who had called him Kelvis said that his clock probably didn't have clockworks but wonder works inside it.

Elvis was giddy with joy. And it was the same every recess from then on. Wherever he went, lots of kids he didn't know came over and joked with him and shouted Felvis and all sorts of other names.

When school was over for the day and Miss Magnusson stood waiting to hear what he wanted to do, whether he wanted to go on or not, he was flaming red in the face and quite dizzy.

"Well?" asked Miss Magnusson.

"Yes," Elvis answered.

"You'll come again?"

"I might as well."

Miss Magnusson thought so too. She'd have a word with the school psychologist and fix everything so there wouldn't be any more misunderstandings. And she'd telephone Mom too.

And so Elvis started school again. But this time he was the one who started. The time before it was Mom; he had only trailed along after her. He hadn't been able to think it all through and he didn't know what he was doing.

That was why he had to stop, obviously, so he could start again, once and for all.

CHAPTER

13

MOM REALLY HAD IT IN for Elvis now.

She was standing at the window. She saw him coming along with his schoolbag, peacefully, as if nothing had happened. She didn't dream that he'd been in school. She thought that he had crept out as usual and run off. She'd phoned all around to ask if anyone had seen him.

First, of course, she called Grandad, in case he might have come into town planning to meet Elvis, because that would have been just like him. But Grandad was home and couldn't tell her anything. Nor could Peter, when she phoned him. No one had seen him. Mom had been terribly worried.

So at first she was relieved when she saw Elvis coming along, but then suddenly she became furious when she noticed his schoolbag and how calmly he took everything.

Because there she'd been, worrying! And there he was with his head in the clouds! He hadn't given her a thought! He thought about everything else but never about his mom!

And why in the world did he want his schoolbag? It wasn't a toy! That meant he'd been rooting around in the coat closet too. Without permission! What a child!

She got so angry that she didn't even shout when she saw him. She just stared.

She was thinking: what is going on inside that head of his anyway? Isn't he ever going to wake up? Will I have to put up with this forever?

Just look at him strolling along! Swinging his bag! Gazing around! But he didn't see her. No sir. She'd been standing there half the day watching for him, beside herself with worry. She hadn't been able to get anything else done. But did he care about that? He wasn't bothered by anything. And she paid a lot of money for that schoolbag and now he probably had ruined it.

Miserable child! she thought, slamming the window shut.

So first Elvis had to hear all about Mom's worrying. But he could feel her anger and reproaches, he didn't have to be told about them. So he couldn't feel much pity for her, though of course he should have. She'd been very worried and all that time she'd been thinking nice thoughts about him. But he couldn't tell that when he got to the door. Then she was just plain bad-tempered.

"Where have you been?"

She grabbed the schoolbag from him.

"Who allowed you to take this out? You're not allowed to have it! What have you got here anyway?"

She opened the schoolbag. The hairpiece! She mustn't see it! Elvis flew at her. He had to stop her finding it.

"What are you up to? Are you trying to fight me?"

Mom gasped for breath with annoyance.

"Let me have my bag!" said Elvis.

"It's not yours!"

"Yes it is!"

"No! Not till you start school, and behave like other people! I'll call the police! You'd better tell me what you've been up to!"

She looked inside the bag but only saw school things. The hairpiece was way at the bottom and she didn't bother to pull things out. Elvis calmed down.

"I've started school," he said.

Mom stared at him.

"What? What're you talking about?"

"I started today," said Elvis.

But Mom didn't believe him.

"You thought that up just so you can have the schoolbag. But you won't get around me that way! I'm not fooled, as you seem to think!"

"Phone Miss Magnusson and ask her," said Elvis. "Go ahead and call her!"

Then Mom started wondering.

"Now what are you up to? You're not allowed to go to school. We decided that you'd wait a year. You don't mean you went and bothered Miss Magnusson? Haven't you already made enough of a nuisance?"

"I didn't bother her!"

Mom had to sit down. This kid really wore her out.

"Answer me! Have you or have you not been to school?"

Of course he had or he wouldn't have said it.

Mom sighed deeply.

"Then I'll have to phone Miss Magnusson right away and apologize."

"No, because Miss Magnusson is going to phone you," said Elvis, absolutely confident, and Mom looked at him dismayed.

"Miss Magnusson is going to phone me? Why?"

"Because I started school. She's going to talk about that."

Mom was all confused. She covered her face with her hands.

All worn out, she repeated, "Miss Magnusson is going to tell me that you've started school?"

"Yes, so you'll know."

"Yes, it would be nice if I knew," Mom said. "Didn't anyone think of asking me what I thought about it? What I wanted? Whether I'd let you go?"

"But you wanted to get rid of me, didn't you?"

"Now don't be insolent! Did you go tell Miss Magnusson that I wanted to get rid of you?"

What a discussion! It made Elvis quite dizzy. Mom wasn't understanding anything, and soon he wouldn't understand anything either. Suddenly it was all just one big muddle. Even though it was really so simple:

He'd been to school.

He could keep on going there.

Miss Magnusson was going to phone Mom and tell her.

That was all set.

But what could he say to make Mom understand?

He tried again. From the very beginning.

"I've started school," he said.

"But you didn't want to," she said.

"Now I do."

"Do you think people can shilly-shally like that? Back and forth? Do you really think so?"

"No, but. . . ."

"Well then!"

"I'm not going to change again."

"That's what you say now! But I have my own opinion. And the school psychologist would certainly agree with me. She knows all about people like you."

Mom talked about the school psychologist with the same tone of voice that she used for the policeman, Elvis noticed. That calmed him down a bit. He knew

all about the policeman and Mom. So maybe he
shouldn't take the school psychologist too seriously either? Miss Magnusson was different. He knew her better than Mom did.

So then Elvis answered in his confident, steady
voice, the one that Mom said always infuriated her.
He said:

"Anyway, Miss Magnusson says I'm allowed to start
school."

"But I didn't! What about me? I'm the one who
decides! Remember that!"

There they were again! They always got to a stone
wall when something had to be explained to Mom. It
felt like being stuck in a traffic jam. And thinking that
you could get out of it by just honking your horn.
Elvis was beside himself.

He had thought that she would be pleased. She
wanted him "out of the way." And he had arranged all
that now. At first he hadn't wanted to, but then he saw
that it would be best this way. He wasn't sorry any
more that she wanted to get rid of him. Sometimes he
wanted to be left alone too. Then he was the one who
wanted to be rid of her. It wasn't anything to fight
about, really. He knew all that now.

But she didn't. She sat there sighing and sighing.

Elvis gave up and went out into the kitchen. He was
thirsty. There were no glasses on the counter so he
climbed up on a chair to reach the shelf.

Then she came out after him.

"Are you going to break some more glasses again?" she asked. "When will you learn to ask permission before you rush for the cupboard?"

She took out a glass and put it down on the counter for him. With a bang.

Elvis took the glass and filled it at the tap. Too much water came much too fast.

"Don't stand there spilling like that! Can't you even fill a glass of water properly?"

What a terrible temper she was in! He watched her movements. She took the glass from him, dried it, filled it with water, put it on the counter.

"There!"

But he wasn't thirsty any more. He could scarcely swallow a single drop.

Mom studied him from top to toe; he could feel it.

"Do you mean to tell me that you went to school looking like that! In those trousers! Do you think those are school clothes? I'm ashamed of you! And did you take that wretched old alarm clock along too? I can hear it ticking. Is that it sticking out of your jacket?"

She looked at him, shaking her head, full of complaints.

"What will your teacher think? It's a reflection on me, don't you see? I'm the one who'll be blamed. You're a disgrace to your mother."

Elvis shook his head too.

"No, because I started school alone today, you know. You weren't along, so I couldn't disgrace you at all."

"Oh yes, when you go to school looking like that, your teacher will think that your mother is a slob."

But Elvis didn't give up. He knew what he was talking about.

"No, because she saw you before, at the roll call. You had the coat on then, so she won't think that at all, you see."

Mom was quiet for a moment. That was true, of course. . . . She had got all dressed up. But still! The child shouldn't wander around looking like this.

"I'll talk to your teacher!" she said.

It sounded like a threat. Elvis went around frightened the rest of the day. A stab of fear hit him every time the phone rang.

But then when Miss Magnusson telephoned later in the evening, nothing special happened. Mom mostly agreed with her.

Yes, of course, Elvis could go to school. That was what she'd wanted all along. All this wasn't her doing at all.

How nice that Miss Magnusson thought everything would be just fine. If not, she should let Mom know. Yes yes, of course. Thank you, thank you. Thank you so very much. I hope he won't be too much trouble. Many many thanks. Thank you.

Yes, that's what it was like now. . . .

Afterward she didn't say a word to Elvis—except that he should make sure that he knew his lesson for tomorrow.

Now all that was set. So why did she have to make such a terrible fuss?

CHAPTER

14

No one came to the door!

Wasn't anyone home?

Elvis stood outside Annarosa's door ringing the bell. He had rung twice, he didn't dare ring again. He stood still and waited.

The hairpiece wrapped in paper was lying in his pocket.

What should he do if no one was home?

Obviously he should wait until they came back, but of course, that might take a long time. . . . Anyway, he had to get rid of the hairpiece now, because otherwise Mom was sure to find it. It was a miracle that she hadn't already. And he couldn't slip it into the mailbox either. Annarosa had a mom too. . . . The whole situation was very frustrating.

He got his courage up and rang a third time. Each time it sounded equally unpleasant, a lonely, echoing buzz inside. His heart leapt inside him when he heard it.

Once he had stood outside the front door at home ringing the same way. That was long ago, when he was little. Mom was mad at him, so he wasn't allowed in. He rang and rang. It was absolutely quiet inside. She didn't answer. All he could hear was the ringing. He got scared. In the end he wondered whether she existed any more, whether she'd died because he was so dumb, whether his home was all empty inside. Perhaps he was going to stand there forever outside until he died too, and no one would ever come.

Then he had heard someone moving around inside and had shouted and knocked on the door as hard as he could, so she had to open up, because of the neighbors, because what would they think if she didn't?

Since then, he always thought it was really awful to hear lonely bells ringing behind locked doors. You could imagine all kinds of. . . .

What if Annarosa didn't exist any more! She hadn't been at school that day, though she had promised. She would have come if she could. Unless something had happened. Something must have happened!

Then he heard a sound from inside. Someone was walking slowly toward the door. He heard the footsteps stop at the other side of the door. And then a voice:

"Who is it?"

Elvis recognized Old Granny. But he couldn't find his voice to speak; it stuck in his throat, because of the door between them.

Old Granny asked again, "Who is it?"

Then he really had to say something. He took the plunge.

"Me," he answered breathlessly.

A while passed. He could hear the rattling of the key and then the door was opened.

"I could hear it was a child's voice," said Old Granny, "otherwise I wouldn't have opened the door."

Elvis asked for Annarosa, but Old Granny was the only one home. She hesitated and then she asked Elvis to come in.

"I shouldn't let anyone in, I promised not to," she said, "but you can't help it with a small child."

"Will Annarosa be back soon?" asked Elvis.

"I don't know, but you can come in and sit for a while if you like."

Elvis followed Old Granny into her room. She walked very slowly now too, and he wondered what she would say if she knew that he had followed her once before. But she didn't know that, and he decided not to tell her. He had learned not to say everything.

Her room was quite big, long and narrow, with a window far away at the opposite narrow end from the door.

Old Granny crossed the room and sat by a little

round table in front of the window. There was another chair on the other side of the table. She pointed to it and told Elvis to sit down.

He did, while he looked around. He was looking for the atlas.

"Are you one of Annarosa's little playmates?" Old Granny asked.

"We're in the same class," Elvis answered.

"Oh, have you started school too? I think you all look so young nowadays when you start school, but that's probably because I'm so very old. Do you know how old I am?"

"No."

"I'll be ninety-four in the spring. If I live that long, probably I won't. I'm going to die quite soon, don't you think?"

Elvis looked at her solemnly. He didn't know what to think.

"It's hard to say for sure," he answered.

Old Granny nodded. Yes, she agreed, it was hard to know for sure.

"But you can guess. . . . They don't understand that here, but then they never understand what I say, so I don't worry about it. If I die, I die. Right?"

Elvis agreed. Not easy to contradict that. He nodded thoughtfully.

"But then again, I might live, and then I'd still have something to worry about," said Old Granny, smiling a little.

Elvis wasn't sure whether she was talking to herself at the moment or to him, because she was staring into space, but the conversation wasn't boring.

"Some things you should put off," he said, "so you have something left."

Elvis had figured that out long ago, that you shouldn't work everything out all at once. He made sure that there was always a little left to think about.

Old Granny turned quickly to face him.

"You see things the same way I do," she said, "but they don't here. It's great fun talking with you."

She sat straight up in her chair and looked delightedly at Elvis. He wondered whether he should ask her about the atlas. He couldn't see it anywhere. But now Old Granny was thinking other thoughts. She talked and he listened. Sometimes his eyes wandered around the room. She must have hidden the atlas. Unless she had got rid of it!

Suddenly he caught sight of something. There were masses of photographs on the bureau. One was of Annarosa; he could tell from a long way off even though she wore her hair differently in the picture, not in two tufts. She had curly hair and it was long. There was a bow like a butterfly on the top of her head. She was wearing a very, very beautiful dress and looked very serious. She was holding a book. The atlas!

Elvis had to walk over to the bureau to see if it really was the atlas.

Yes, no doubt about it.

"Where are you off to, my little friend?" asked Old Granny, watching him.

Elvis took the picture from the bureau and walked over to where she was sitting. He pointed to the atlas.

"That's an atlas," he said to Old Granny.

"Yes, that it is," she said. "And I can tell you, I still have that atlas. But the girl in the picture—she doesn't exist any more."

Elvis felt cold all over.

Annarosa! She didn't exist any more! Everything went blurry before his eyes. Something had happened to her after all. Beside himself with grief, he looked at Old Granny. But she wasn't looking at him; she was staring at the girl in the picture.

"She's gone, forever," she said, her fingers trembling.

"Where is she?" Elvis asked in a thick voice.

"Gone," said Old Granny. "And she didn't vanish yesterday either. . . ."

"But I saw her yesterday!" cried Elvis, all confused.

Old Granny looked at him, but her eyes wandered on further, past him.

"Did you?" she said; it sounded as if she didn't believe him.

"Yes. I talked with her. I was here yesterday!" Elvis said.

Old Granny shook her head, smiling slightly.

"Don't talk nonsense," she said, looking stubborn. "You thought you talked with her, but you saw someone completely different. Besides, I can't remember having met you before. You say that you were here yesterday?"

"Yes, for sure. And I know that it was Annarosa."

Old Granny put the picture down on the table.

"Annarosa, yes," she said, almost scolding. "But this isn't Annarosa. . . . This is myself when I was a child."

Elvis took a deep breath. He looked at Old Granny. Then he picked up the photograph and looked at it very carefully. He was relieved. It took a while before he really saw that it wasn't Annarosa. Suddenly he did see, but what the difference was exactly, except for the hair, he couldn't exactly say. It was more like an unreal Annarosa in the picture, as if she were very, very far away.

"That she is," whispered Old Granny. "Terribly, terribly far away."

Elvis looked at her shyly.

"Now maybe you understand what I mean when I say that the girl in the picture disappeared," she said, "very long ago."

"Far away is not the same thing as disappeared," said Elvis, shaking his head.

Then Old Granny smiled, but she said that he was right. Elvis pointed to the atlas in the picture again.

"Where is the atlas?" he asked.

"In the top drawer of the bureau, if you'd like to have a look at it. You can get it yourself. Will you put the picture back at the same time?"

Elvis did as she said. And now he was holding the atlas. It was the first time he had ever held anything so remarkable. A book with the whole world inside it.

"They say that the world doesn't look like this nowadays," Old Granny said tonelessly. "Well, it may have changed as much as I have myself, for all I know; that's something you can't be sure of. Perhaps it is disappearing too."

"No!" cried Elvis. "The world isn't going to disappear."

"That's good to hear," said Old Granny.

Then they leafed through the atlas together, and Old Granny told Elvis the names of all the islands she saw. She'd always thought that the islands in the world were the most important things to remember, and she knew most of them by heart. She was very bright. There were lots of islands and time passed swiftly.

Suddenly she looked up from the atlas and asked Elvis:

"My dear, can you see whether the door over there is open?"

"Which door?" Elvis asked. He thought that she meant the door in some other room. But she meant the door to her own room, and he was startled.

Couldn't she see that it was closed? Was her eyesight that bad? Poor thing. . . .

So that she wouldn't know how poor her eyes were, compared with his, and be sad about it, Elvis got up and went over to the door and looked. He pretended that he didn't see very well either.

"No, it is closed," he said.

Then Old Granny smiled.

"But dear child, surely your eyesight isn't that bad at your age, is it?"

Elvis didn't answer. Did she realize that he was only pretending? She was still smiling, as if she were about to laugh.

"That was sweet of you," she said. "Very sweet."

He didn't know what she meant or in what way he had been sweet. He felt sort of ashamed and unsure. Because it was wrong to pretend like that. . . .

But then they started looking at the atlas again and he forgot all about it.

After a while Old Granny looked up again.

"Now they'll be back soon," she said. "I heard them."

Elvis listened but he didn't hear anything. He looked at her questioningly.

"I always get a premonition about them," said Old Granny. "That means that I hear them put the key in the lock about ten minutes before they come. I just heard it, so now we know that they are on their way."

Elvis looked at her, full of amazement. Just think, she had such good hearing, much better than his, even though she was so very old. So perhaps she wasn't too upset about her eyesight. Perhaps one equaled the other. . . .

She said:

"When you're old, it can be more important to hear than to see. You probably can't understand that, but I think I've seen almost everything there is to see. And I'll never have done with hearing."

Just then Elvis heard something. Quite right! A key rattled in the outside door.

"Now!" he said. "Here they are!"

"Right," said Old Granny. "I didn't hear that, but after all, I knew it already. . . ."

At that very moment Annarosa entered the room.

CHAPTER

15

THAT DAY Annarosa looked very much like the girl on Old Granny's bureau, probably because she looked more serious than usual. He could tell that she was thinking about something different from the others. She looked rather pale too. Maybe that was because she hadn't been to school.

"Are you ill?" Elvis asked her.

She just shook her head.

Then her mom came and asked if anyone had rung the doorbell.

"Only this little boy," said Old Granny.

"But I told you not to open the door," said Mom. She sounded stern and seemed worried. She nodded curtly to Elvis. Maybe she didn't like him being there?

Old Granny defended herself, "I asked who it was first."

But that didn't help.

"That's the same as saying someone is home," said Mom. "Next time you'll do as I say."

"I can usually tell if it's something bad," Old Granny said. "This time I knew it was something nice."

She nodded in a friendly way several times to Elvis.

"You and your ideas!" Mom swept out of the room.

There was a kind of uneasiness in the air that day. Elvis knew all about that mood from home. And Annarosa looked depressed. He knew exactly how she felt. But Old Granny was her usual self; she smiled at them and it was as if she read Elvis' thoughts when she said:

"At my age, despite everything, it's better to be treated like a five-year-old than someone almost a hundred. I mean there's some hope for someone who is five. . . ."

She laughed. Elvis laughed too, but Annarosa stayed serious and said nothing. She wasn't happy that day.

Then Mom came back. She had put soft drinks and pastries out for them all in the kitchen. They went in there after her. She filled the glasses and cut slices of jelly roll. She joked and chatted; she'd changed her mood.

Annarosa became slightly happier too.

Then Mom disappeared into the living room to water the flowers.

Finally Elvis could give the hairpiece back to Anna-

rosa. She hid it right away, but didn't ask him anything about how it went or whether he had started
school. Nothing!

Had she forgotten all about it? Maybe she didn't
care what happened?

"I was in school today," said Elvis.

"Yes," was all she said. A little yes, nothing more.

"But you weren't there."

"No!"

Just as short. She put a pile of cookies into her
mouth all at once and told Elvis to do the same. But
he wouldn't have been able to force down a crumb at
that moment.

"I stuck on the hair," he whispered.

She nodded with all the cookies in her mouth.

"You couldn't see it under my cap."

She nodded again with her mouth full. She didn't
look quite as interested as he would have liked. But he
told her what happened anyway, that he forgot to take
his cap off carefully, and the hairpiece came off with it.
Then she woke up a bit.

"That was silly! Then they could see your stubble,"
she said.

Elvis nodded but didn't seem too upset by his
clumsiness.

"Did Miss Magnusson see it?" Annarosa asked.

"Sure she did, but it didn't matter. I can have it in
school."

"The hairpiece?"

"No, the stubble."

"Weird. But the school psychologist said. . . ."

"That was a mistake," explained Elvis. "I can go to school now. According to Mom too."

Annarosa took some long swallows of her soft drink; she drank and drank, her eyes staring at the opposite wall. Suddenly it seemed as if she didn't care whether he was allowed to go to school or not. Even though she did care yesterday. She was so eager then. She had told him that he absolutely had to start again.

He didn't know what more to say. So he started drinking his soft drink too. And he noticed that when you really begin, you can drink any old amount. So there they sat facing each other, staring at the walls behind each other's backs, gulping down the soft drinks, glass after glass, without a word.

Mom came out into the kitchen and joked with them again. A great deal. Very loudly. Every single word she used was a joke.

Elvis didn't really take part, but Annarosa laughed, and it was good that she wasn't sad any more. But instead he felt as if he were the one who was becoming gloomy in some way he couldn't explain. Peter often joked, but that made him happy, and now he was uneasy and anxious.

Suddenly he felt that he had drunk too much and he had to rush to the bathroom.

Just when he started peeing, the door opened and there stood Annarosa. She had to go too. But he couldn't stop right in the middle. And she didn't go away. She stayed right there. He didn't look at her, but he felt her watching him. And suddenly he heard her shout:

"Mom! Come here a minute! Look!"

Elvis felt hot. He heard her mom's footsteps.

"Come see the really neat way he pees!" Annarosa shouted in delight.

At last he was finished. Her mom, as luck would have it, didn't bother to look.

"But honey, all boys pee like that. Didn't you know that?" was all she said.

She didn't sound very impressed.

Elvis didn't dare look at Annarosa.

No one had said "really neat" about anything he did ever before. And even though he knew that it wasn't so special, he was quite happy. But he was surprised too. And why did her mom have to say that all boys pee like that? Even though it was true, he felt a little foolish.

He still didn't dare look at Annarosa.

Then he felt her hand on his stubble.

"It's great that you can start school," she said. She smiled and said that his stubble felt soft, softer than the hairpiece. Now her eyes were the way they used to be. Before, it was as if they didn't fit as well into his as they had on other days, but now they did again.

Then a frown came between her eyebrows and she looked thoughtful.

"Mom is so dumb," she said. "Of course I know how boys pee, but anyway you pee best of all—so there!"

"It was nothing," said Elvis modestly. "Are you coming to school tomorrow?"

She nodded, but turned quite serious again.

"Soon perhaps I'll have to go to another school," she said. "We're probably moving. Mom thinks so."

She explained that yesterday drunken Enar had come over again and fought and made a scene all night long. He wouldn't leave Mom alone. They couldn't get rid of him.

"He's like a burr, you see," said Annarosa.

"A burr?" Elvis listened carefully. "Like the ones that stick on you?" he asked.

"Exactly," Annarosa nodded gloomily. They hadn't been able to get rid of him until Granny went to the store. Then Mom phoned Johnny, the one she might marry, and told him all about it. Then Johnny came over in his car and he thought that Mom should marry him right away, so that he could cut Enar right out of her life in case he turned up again. Mom said she wasn't sure. And then they drove off in the car to another town and looked at a place to live, where they would go if they moved.

But Annarosa didn't want to. She wanted to stay where they were.

Neither Granny nor Old Granny would go along with them if they moved. Of course, she could come visit them sometimes, but Annarosa couldn't go to the same school either. She would have to go to the one in the other town.

Just because of drunken Enar. Otherwise Mom wouldn't get married. She didn't want to stop working at the restaurant. Everything was fine the way it was.

Johnny was quite boring. Enar was much more fun if only he didn't get so terribly drunk, because then he got really dumb and noisy and made trouble.

Last night he sat down in the hall and wouldn't let anyone pass him. When Annarosa was supposed to go to school, he wouldn't let her out. She thought of climbing out the window, but it was too high. She might have broken her leg. So all she could do was wait until he went away.

Then he wanted to go out after breakfast, but Mom said that she had to come along and look at the apartment.

That was why she hadn't been in school today. She hadn't been able to get there. And now no one knew what was going to happen. . . .

Everything depended on drunken Enar.

Now Mom came out into the kitchen again. And Granny too. They had been watching TV. Annarosa suddenly stopped talking.

"How solemn you look, my dears! Is something terribly wrong?" Granny asked.

"We were just talking about school," Annarosa answered, in order to say something.

"Oh? Isn't it going well?"

Granny looked concerned. She was being kind and wanted to find out what was the matter. This could be awkward. They didn't know what to say, but she wouldn't give up.

"Is it your teacher? Is she difficult?"

"Maybe," answered Annarosa weakly.

"How? Tell me so I'll know," said Granny.

Elvis shook his head seriously.

"No, not Miss Magnusson," he said. "She's good."

"Then what's the trouble?"

Granny looked hard from one to the other. They looked at each other unhappily. Mom was fussing with the dishes at the sink and wasn't interested in what they were talking about.

"Come on," said Granny. "Tell me what's bothering you."

What could they answer?

"Oh, it's nothing," they said both at once.

"Oh, yes, something must be the matter."

It wasn't going to be easy to get out of this. Both of them struggled as best they could to think up a good worry, one that wouldn't be dangerous to talk about. Elvis figured one out first.

"She isn't our real teacher," he said.

"No," Annarosa chimed in. "She's just a substitute."

"Now I understand," said Granny. "You're sorry because you can't keep her. That's a pity. . . ."

Yes, it was sad. Annarosa and Elvis thought so too. Lots of things were sad, in fact.

On the way home Elvis thought about one sad thing and then another. . . .

But suddenly he felt quite happy. Think of what Annarosa said to him in the bathroom! What luck that no one at home had heard that!

Mom, for instance, she always got so shy and angry about things like that! Lucky she wasn't around.

CHAPTER

16

JUST IMAGINE—Elvis had started fighting with Miss Magnusson. That was something he never thought he would ever do.

No one else fought; he was the only one, and in the beginning he didn't either. But after he'd gone to school for a good number of days, so many that he couldn't keep count of them, he suddenly started doing the very opposite of what Miss Magnusson said. He didn't know why. It just happened that way.

It wasn't because he thought Miss Magnusson was dumb or because he wanted to be clever; he just couldn't help it.

He did foolish things—contradicted, wrote numbers when they were supposed to write letters, read the wrong page, talked loudly during singing, and lots of other silly things.

If only he could figure out why.

Because it really wasn't much fun—and Miss Magnusson didn't notice any of it. She didn't pay the slightest attention to him now. She did on that first day: then she looked and talked right at him. But not any more. Now she looked at all the others just as much. No matter what he came up with, she didn't care at all. Didn't care about him in the slightest. It was as if he didn't exist.

So he didn't understand why she wanted to have him in school at all. It would have been better if she'd told him that in the first place, that he needn't start again because she wasn't going to notice him anyway.

Those were gloomy, wasted days. Outside it rained and inside no sunshine shone on the desk top.

Annarosa still stayed with the girls during recess. And he didn't know if he could be with the boys. Probably he could, but he wasn't sure he really wanted to. Usually, big kids came and joked with him during recess so he wasn't all alone. He didn't have a bad time, but in the end it got quite tricky, all that joking; he played the monkey, they made him their pet, but it didn't feel right any more.

He didn't regret starting school, not at all. He wanted to go on even though he had to sit all the time, and so little happened, and everyone had to do the same thing at the same time. Even though they sang too, because that hadn't got any better; they still sang every single day, and he made even more of a nuisance of himself then, though Miss Magnusson didn't notice. Nothing helped.

But then one day, when he had been extra difficult and a noisy troublemaker, so that he had got quite tired, suddenly Miss Magnusson was standing right in front of him.

"Why are you acting like this, Elvis?" she asked.

He got all confused and couldn't answer.

But she repeated the question again:

"Elvis, why are you acting like this?"

Her eyes were serious but not angry, not even scolding. She wanted to know why, just what she asked.

So that was why Elvis told her that he wasn't used to sitting in the same spot and doing the same things every day.

"But that's the way it is in school," said Miss Magnusson, and she wasn't the one who thought it up. And he had been able to choose whether or not he wanted to start again: he knew what he was getting in for.

Had he changed his mind again?

Did he want to stop? Is that why he was acting this way?

Elvis shook his head. No, he wanted to go on.

"Are you going to go on making trouble too?" Miss Magnusson asked calmly.

Elvis didn't answer.

Miss Magnusson looked at him with her clear eyes and said in her clear voice:

"I'm making you sad, Elvis, I know. But there's really nothing I can do about it, even though I really wish I could."

She was silent for a while, gazing at him.

Elvis kept quiet too, but he listened—both to her words and to her silence.

"There must be a better way," she said, "than just to be contrary. Don't you think?"

She was asking a serious question and she wanted an answer. Elvis noticed that, so he answered that he would think about it.

"I don't know right now, you see," he said. "I'll have to think about it first."

And she understood that, but she was sure he would come up with something. She knew that he had to have some reason for making trouble, that he didn't do it only to make a nuisance of himself. That was why she wanted to talk with him, she said, because she was counting on him to work it out, when he had finished thinking about it.

Yes, Elvis thought he could.

"But the singing is the worst," he said. "What'll we do about that?"

"Well, you can do what you want about it," said Miss Magnusson. "You usually don't sing anyway."

But she thought he might stop talking loudly while

the others sang, because most of the class enjoyed singing and they shouldn't have to give it up just because
he didn't want to.

No, of course—as long as he could get out of it himself then. . . .

Then Miss Magnusson laughed and looked exactly
the way she did the first day.

"I'd like to see the person who tried to force you,"
she said. "As long as you do everything else, naturally
you don't have to sing. It isn't the most important
thing in the world."

She left it up to him to decide whether he wanted to
or not.

"But one fine day maybe you'll start singing too,
Elvis," she said, smiling.

Then she walked away.

Elvis stayed there awhile wondering why she
couldn't be their real teacher. Mightn't there be some
mistake—perhaps the other one who was coming after
Christmas was the substitute instead?

He had to figure out a way to stop being contrary. . . .

But it didn't take a lot of brain power this time,
strangely enough. The need to be a nuisance just vanished by itself. Almost without his noticing it.

Before, he had thought that he was wasting every
day, one after the other. Now not a single day was lost,
even though it was often raining outside and they had

to sit in the same seats and do the same things all the time—and the sun never shone on his desk top. It wouldn't until next year, Miss Magnusson said, because now the sun was much too low in the sky; its light couldn't reach in through the window.

But it would be back in the spring, in the spring when they would get their real teacher. But it wouldn't matter then. He'd rather give up the sun on his desk and keep the substitute teacher. Or else he would leave when she did. Especially if Annarosa was going to move too.

What Miss Magnusson said to him—"I'm making you sad, Elvis, I know. But there's really nothing I can do about it, even though I really wish I could"—he thought about those words very often. Because when you say something like that, it means that you understand lots of things that people don't usually think about, things everyone should understand but that are quite impossible to explain. . . .

So now he didn't have to be noisy and contrary any more.

One day when he came back from school, Mom was talking on the phone and laughing. She nodded to Elvis and winked and said that he was "too cute for words." Then she laughed again. He could hear one of her girl friends on the other end of the line. Mom listened and laughed and cocked her head to one side and looked at Elvis.

What was this all about? She had that moony voice she used when she was talking about the real ELVIS, but now she was talking about him!

"Yes, imagine, it's so cute, isn't it! He's not demonstrative at all, you'd never think he would. Maybe he's starting to develop some feelings, who knows. . . ."

Then she burst into laughter again and went on:

"I wonder what his teacher would say if she knew."

Elvis stared at her blankly. She winked at him again.

Teacher? . . . Knew? . . . What?

What were they talking about?

Then he caught sight of a letter on the telephone table. It was sticking out of an envelope. He rushed over and grabbed it.

It was his own private letter that he had written to Miss Magnusson, and no one in the whole world was to see it!

So Mom had been poking around in his things again! She'd found the envelope that he had hidden so carefully. She'd ripped it open and read his letter. And that wasn't all! She had phoned her friends too and read it to them, so now everyone knew. . . . Now they were sitting there, laughing. . . .

"Can you believe it! He's just grabbed the letter away from me!" Mom said into the phone, giggling. "And he looks so angry that I'm getting scared."

She was reporting everything he did.

"Now he's blushing too! Yes ... poor fellow, so worked up ... yes, you know how kids are. ..."

It was all just sweet, cute and adorable, nothing for him to be ashamed of.

Then she recited what was in the letter. She said she knew it by heart, Elvis' first love letter; she'd store it in her memory and never forget it, and then she recited it in that moony voice:

"Dearest Substitute! I love you Miss Magnusson. I want to marry you Miss Magnusson. But later. Not now. With best wishes from your loving Elvis Karlsson."

And then they laughed and laughed and laughed.

Elvis tore the letter into little tiny pieces.

Mom caught him at it, dropped the phone and tried to stop him. She said that she wanted to keep it for him so that he would have something to laugh about when he grew up, because then he'd understand how funny it was.

But Elvis turned away from her.

What did she know about when he grew up?

What would she know then? What did she know now?

What did she know at all?

All that was left of the letter were tiny white flakes, a handful of bits of scribbles that he caught up in his hand and threw in her face so that they fluttered like a cloud of snow past her frightened eyes.

Then he rushed away. And he had never run in all

his life as fast as he ran away from home right then.

He would never come back! Never! Never again!

He ran as far as he dared. He didn't want to meet anyone. He just wanted to be alone and not think about anything.

It got dark. And cold. And it started to rain.

He became wet and cold.

Then Dad drove up in the car. He slowed down and stopped. The headlights shone on the asphalt. Dad didn't shout. He climbed out and fetched Elvis, didn't say a word, just patted him on the back.

Elvis was so tired that he just went along with him. He wasn't up to doing anything else. Everything had turned black and cold around him—and he had no-where to go.

Dad wasn't angry, just scared. And Mom cried when

they got home. She wasn't angry either. But she didn't understand why she had such a strange child, she said, sniffling, she would never understand Elvis.

"It doesn't matter," said Elvis to comfort her.

She needn't be sad because she didn't understand him, because now there were other people who did. He could really look after himself.

But Mom cried anyway. She said that he could scare the living daylights out of her.

All she wanted to do was tell about how cute he was. . . .

Now that for once he had been quite cute. . . .

And then he went and acted like this. . . .

CHAPTER

17

Mom told Elvis that she snooped in his hiding places for his own good. All mothers have to snoop, because otherwise kids get up to all sorts of crazy things. Kids have to be protected from getting carried away, so that mothers won't be disgraced.

It's their duty to snoop and pry in their kids' things, and kids should be grateful, but they never are. Especially pigheaded ones like Elvis who never know their own good.

She said that she was always anxious about him.

Kids shouldn't keep any secrets from their parents. They have no right to hide anything, especially from their mothers. Because if they do, how can their mothers help them when something bad happens to them?

"But you don't have to help me, see!" said Elvis, and then once again Mom thought that he looked like one of those stubborn little brown calves she remembered from her childhood, that no one could control.

She never got anything out of him when he came home from school. She could never get any clear answers.

He just stood there, staring and squirming.

And there's so much a mother wonders about, so much she has to know—yes, that she *has the right* to know! But she never got an answer to even the simplest questions, like, for example:

"How was school today, Elvis?"

"What classes did you have?"

"What did Miss Magnusson say?"

And how did he get on with his schoolmates?

Who were his best friends?

What did so-and-so's dad do? What did his mom look like? Had Elvis been over to their home? What kind of a car did they have? Did they have a summer place? A color TV? Why didn't he play with that boy instead? Or the other one?

And why didn't he ever bring any friends home? So that she could meet them. Didn't he know that he could? She would get lots of treats to offer them. Wouldn't that be great fun?

Didn't he realize she wondered who he was going around with when he didn't come straight home after school? Didn't he realize that she wasn't that dumb? Of course she knew that he went over to someone's house. Who was it? Whose house did he go to every day?

That was what Elvis heard as soon as he got to the

front door. The same torrent of questions every time. Sometimes he really tried to answer her. But it never worked out—as soon as he answered one question, a hundred new ones popped up. Mom could think up more strange questions than anyone else. Dad agreed: he couldn't cope with them either.

As for Mom, she said that she had no secrets from anyone. She made it sound as if secrets were ugly, shameful. She really believed that he didn't want to tell because he was ashamed.

Elvis had only one real secret, and that was the one inside him. He couldn't talk about that at all. Mom wouldn't want to hear about it either, because it wasn't her kind of thing.

Then there were a whole lot of things he didn't tell because it wasn't necessary, and they weren't even secrets, though she thought they were. They were just things that he kept to himself for one reason or other. But he couldn't get that across to her. She thought that she had the right to know everything about him since she was his mother.

That was why she didn't give up until she found out what she wanted to know. If she couldn't get it out of Elvis, she'd find it out some other way.

One day when Elvis strolled up to the front door, he heard:

"So, Elvis, you're seeing Annarosa Pettersson, are you? I heard that today from Siv."

He turned away and didn't answer her.

Mom went on, "Now I want to know if what my friend Siv told me is true. Are you hanging around with Annarosa Pettersson every day? Yes or no! Answer me!"

But Elvis didn't want to start a whole discussion about Annarosa, so he didn't let on, just took a cracker and filled his mouth with it. Why was she asking anyway, since she already knew?

"Oh, so you're even ashamed to admit it?" Mom said, opening her eyes wide as she stared at him.

"No!" said Elvis emphatically.

What did she mean? Why should he be ashamed?

He had to find that out anyway.

Naturally he'd managed to pick the one person in his whole class that Mom didn't want him to be with. She should have expected as much. It was stupid of her not to.

Elvis didn't get it. . . . What did Mom know about Annarosa? Did she know her?

"No! What do you think? I don't go around with that kind of people," said Mom.

Well, then, how could she say anything about them?

"You don't have to stick your nose in filth to know it smells," she said. And then Elvis had to listen to what kind of people Annarosa and her mom were. And her granny too.

They were bad people. Her mom had children everywhere: other people were bringing them up. She couldn't look after them herself. Annarosa's granny had been just the same. So Annarosa couldn't possibly be well brought up. They let her run wild. No supervision, no discipline at all. So if he really wanted to get into trouble, all he had to do was keep on visiting that house.

They had bad habits too, drunken parties until dawn; their neighbors knew that all too well, they could never get to sleep because of the noise. And Annarosa was allowed to stay up, so it was obvious what would happen to the child.

"It's very sad, Elvis, that you have such bad taste that you didn't notice this," said Mom.

Then Elvis interrupted her flow of words. Because he knew more about all this than Mom. Annarosa didn't usually go to the parties.

"She sleeps in Old Granny's room then!" he said.

Mom opened her eyes wide and stared at him.

"Oh, so you know what kind of life they lead and still you go around with the girl?" she said. "This is worse than I thought, Elvis."

"Of course I know," said Elvis, "since we're friends, and there's nothing wrong with them."

Mom was saying nothing but lies, lies and gossip and nonsense. It made him furious.

"I really think Siv knows more about this than you do, Elvis dear," said Mom sarcastically.

Elvis couldn't control himself any more.

"Blabbermouths!" he shouted.

That was the last straw for Mom. She ordered Elvis off into the bedroom. He couldn't go outside any more that day. Moreover, she said that he couldn't see Annarosa any more, but he decided not to really worry about that. He would get back at her.

"Then I forbid you to see Siv any more!" Elvis shouted. "Because you're so nasty when you're with her."

Mom had just said that he got nasty from seeing Annarosa. She was allowed to say things like that but he wasn't. She started to whine about how terrible he was to her. And when Dad got home, she told him all about it.

But Dad didn't completely agree with her, you could tell; he just pretended so that there wouldn't be any more fighting. That was often the way it was. All he said was:

"You heard what Mom said, Elvis!"

That was all he had to say, but he repeated it a good many times.

"Isn't that typical?" said Mom. "When he finally starts playing with kids his own age, he chooses someone that no one else wants to be with. Why can't he play with boys just as well? Wouldn't that be more natural?"

"Sure. Listen to what Mom says, Elvis," Dad repeated.

To end the discussion, Elvis promised to start playing with the boys in his class.

The very next day he came home trailing a whole
lot of boys.

"You can come home with me today," he said to one
boy after another.

Everyone who could came along, and it was quite a
crowd.

He thought, Well, now Mom is going to be really
pleased when she has so many to look over. It's better
to bring them all at once, then perhaps I can have a
little peace and quiet.

At first Mom looked a bit odd, seeing him followed
by so many boys. She didn't have enough snacks at
home! But then she pulled herself together and said
hello to them all in a friendly way. Then she took
Princess and ran out to buy more pastries. On the way
she met a couple of ladies she had to chat with, so she
ended up being away a long time.

Meanwhile the boys wandered around the place,
and Elvis showed them all his possessions. Just the way
Mom did when guests came over who hadn't been
there before.

Actually he thought it felt phony but he couldn't
think of anything else to do. He wasn't used to having
guests.

When one of the boys said that he liked a little car
that Elvis had, Elvis swiftly replied:

"You can have it!"

The boy hesitated; it was a great car; he wouldn't have given it away himself. . . .

"Sure, take it! I don't want it," Elvis said, shoving the car at him.

Right afterward another boy liked another car.

"You can have it!" Elvis said immediately.

Then all the boys discovered, one after the other, that they all liked Elvis' toys incredibly much. The same thing was repeated every time. Elvis gave away his toys, one after the other. Sometimes someone would wonder if it wasn't all getting out of hand, but Elvis stood by what he said and each boy had to accept the gift.

Elvis was red in the face and excited—perhaps he didn't really know what he was doing—but giving things away was fun; he couldn't stop himself. Showing his belongings had taken on an unexpected importance.

He only hesitated over Johan's things. He couldn't give them away. He felt that they owned them together, he and Johan, so he didn't give them away to anyone.

"That belongs to Johan," he said to the boys, and they quickly learned what that meant. They touched Johan's things with careful hands and put them carefully back where they belonged.

They knew perfectly well what was possible and what wasn't.

The piggy bank, for example. Despite the fact that it was high up on a shelf, they saw right off that it was within the limits of possibility.

They pointed to it.

"Whose is that? Is it yours?"

Elvis swiftly climbed up to get the piggy bank, took it down and put it on the kitchen table.

One of the boys touched it, shook it and listened.

"How heavy it is! It's really full!"

"Do you have lots of money?"

They all looked at him. Lots of money! Their eyes glittered.

"Have you counted it all?"

No, he hadn't. He had no idea. . . .

The piggy bank was passed from hand to hand. They shook it and listened to the clinking of coins. They all looked at Elvis but said nothing.

Then he understood. He got a knife. Mom had put a new plug in the bottom, because the other one had been too easy to pick out. This one fitted tighter. But he could get it out with the knife. And the boys' help.

Soon the money was rolling out all over the table and down onto the floor.

The boys threw themselves upon it. They helped hunt down every single penny. When they were about to hand it all back to him, he simply said:

"No, keep it. You can!"

They hesitated. After all, money is money!

"No! I want you to have it!"

"But—shouldn't we count the money?" someone asked.

"No, we don't have to. . . ."

Elvis divided up the money. He stuffed some into the pockets of those who didn't take any by themselves. They made weak little sounds of protest that they didn't really mean. Elvis was all worked up and excited. This was really fun.

The empty piggy bank was put back up on the shelf again. It would be a long time before it rattled so cheerily again. It stood there silent and empty. But Elvis thought that it looked happier than it did before.

Now it had a chance to be liked for its own sake again, not just because of the money.

The boys looked at him; they stood around in the kitchen gently jingling the coins in their pockets.

Suddenly Elvis discovered that he didn't have anything more to show them. He looked all around. No—in fact—he had shown them everything.

"Mom will be back soon with snacks," he said.

Right. . . . The boys' eyes moved uneasily toward the door.

"I have to go soon," one of them said.

"Me too!" said another.

"Me too!"

"Don't you want any cakes?" Elvis asked. "And juice?"

No, they weren't very hungry. . . . Besides, soon it would be suppertime. And their mothers were probably waiting for them. . . .

They had to be off now. All of them.

"Bye then!" said Elvis.

He stood at the window, waving to them.

Yes, he could see that they were in a great hurry; they ran as fast as they could in every direction. He understood. He knew what it was like to be late for supper.

Right afterward, Mom came in with a big bag of sweet buns.

"Where have they all gone?" she asked.

"They've already left," said Elvis, gesturing with his hands.

"Will they be back?" asked Mom. "I got slightly delayed. I didn't know they were in such a rush."

No, they wouldn't be coming back.

"They're gone," said Elvis, stretching out his hands again.

"You look strange! What have you been up to?"

Mom looked around the place.

"Something else has gone from here too, I see!" she said suspiciously. Then she looked everywhere and discovered one thing after another that was missing.

Elvis stayed in the kitchen. He just sat there. Strangely his whole self went numb.

He heard Mom's startled shout when she discovered that everything was gone. But he didn't pay any attention. He noticed that Mom had opened the bag of buns. He felt as if the whole kitchen were full of buns. Now she came in and the discussion started.

"Elvis, you have absolutely no instinct for self-preservation!" she said.

At first he didn't take in what she said—just some more words he couldn't really understand.

But then she started sobbing and saying the same thing over and over. So then he finally caught on.

Self-preservation was something he didn't have, that everyone needed to get along. What could it be?

Something made him think of an *Alexander cake* when he heard the words.

They usually had an Alexander cake at Easter time. It tasted creamy, wafery and good but it made you feel quite full. Self-preservation sounded just as rich and satisfying somehow.

So how do you go about getting it?

He giggled a little.

Do you bake it yourself or order it from the store?

"This is not a laughing matter," Mom said gloomily, taking the buns out of the paper bag. "It's really very sad, Elvis, to have no instinct for self-preservation. I can't imagine what will happen to you when you grow up."

CHAPTER

18

THE TIME OF YEAR had come when Santa could expect a message any minute from Mom about how Elvis was behaving.

Christmas was just around the corner.

Christmas meant a lot to Mom. That was why she cleaned and worked so hard around the house. She said that she wanted a real Christmas, but they never had one, because neither Elvis nor Dad had any Christmas spirit.

Dad just sat around in front of the TV, watching ice hockey matches, and Elvis didn't show much interest either.

It certainly was very strange! Kids are supposed to be full of expectation at that season, their eyes glowing like stars before the wonder of Christmas, said Mom, but Elvis hadn't even got around to making a list of what he wanted so that she could tell Grandma and everyone else who asked what to give him.

Other kids were nice and obedient just before
Christmas, but Elvis was difficult as ever. He just
stared at her and gave her a funny look when she
threatened to phone Santa and tell him not to give
Elvis any presents.

No, Elvis certainly didn't have much Christmas
spirit.

The only one who really did something about
Christmas, who nearly worked herself to death to make
everything nice, was Mom, but she got little thanks for
her slaving! Besides, who gave a thought to what
would make her happy?

"What if you both tried just this once?" she would
say. "Or is that too much to ask?"

Christmas always ended up being a lot of hard work
and trouble for her, never a pleasant surprise. She
didn't expect anything for herself from it, not in the
slightest, though she did everything for them.

Elvis had heard it all before, but this was the first
time he took it seriously. Miss Magnusson said that the
point of Christmas was for everyone to make each
other happy. No one should ever end up being sad.

But that was just what happened to Mom—she went
around feeling sad. He realized that now. She hadn't
been happy all autumn long. It wasn't all his fault
either. He had tried hard to be good, though she
hadn't noticed. He obeyed her if he could--that is, if
she was right. But if she was wrong, then he really

couldn't. Because he did have to obey himself too, and she never considered that. He often had much more difficult problems than she would ever be able to understand.

Perhaps he ought to feel sorry for Mom. . . .

She always used to be happy when she played her ELVIS records; she used to sing and dance along, but now she just sat around. She could play the same song over and over without getting happy.

She used to play with Princess all the time, but she didn't any more. She never petted her. She behaved differently toward Princess and he could tell it made Princess unhappy. She hung around Mom quietly with adoring eyes but only got shoved aside. Mom used to pay a lot of attention to her before, and now, of course, Princess couldn't understand why she had changed.

"Dogs are no fun when they get big. I don't want her around any more," said Mom.

She hardly ever wanted to let her in the house. She thought Princess smelled "doggy." She was tired of Princess and never took her for walks; Dad and Elvis had to do that. Elvis really felt terribly sorry for Princess. . . .

But maybe if Mom had a real Christmas she would be happy again!

Something had to be done. At least for Princess' sake.

What if they could think up a surprise for Mom! That would be great!

Elvis talked to Dad about it, but he dismissed the idea.

"I can't afford it," he said. "We haven't paid for the color TV yet."

They should have waited to get that for Christmas, the way he wanted. Then that could have been their surprise, said Dad.

"But then, you see, she wouldn't have got to watch the real ELVIS," said Elvis.

"Too bad. Anyway I can't afford any surprises now."

Dad didn't want to hear any more about it.

And as for Elvis, he had given away all the money in his piggy bank. He wished he had it now. It was a shame he didn't.

But Mom had to have a surprise anyway—one way or another.

He knew that she had longed for a ring for ages.

Her girl friend Mai had been given a ring last Christmas and Inga got one on her wedding anniversary and Siv on her birthday. Mom was the only one who hadn't got one. And always whenever Elvis went out with her, she would stop in front of the jewelry stores. She could stand there for ages, looking in the window.

Ordinarily Elvis thought this was boring. He usu-

ally went off and did something else meanwhile, but now he started being interested.

He went out with Mom willingly. Every time they passed a jeweler, he stopped. But naturally—wasn't it always that way?—now Mom walked right past the jewelers. She didn't have time to stand around in the Christmas rush.

"Besides, what good does it do? When you can't have even the tiniest pearl?" she said, dragging Elvis along with her.

The tiniest pearl!

That was good to know! So she wanted a ring with a pearl, not one of those with different-colored shiny stones. Now he knew.

Another question was whether she wanted several

small pearls or just one big one. He tried every possible way to get Mom to give her opinion, but she just stared at him blankly.

"What's come over you? You're not interested in jewelry."

Elvis almost gave up the whole plan. Especially when he heard Mom tell Grandma on the phone that obviously Elvis was planning to buy Miss Magnusson a ring for Christmas—because he was so much in love with her, said Mom. And then they laughed at him again.

Then it was really touch and go whether Mom would get her ring, but he controlled himself. There was no point in getting angry. Better instead to get the ring as soon as possible, before he regretted it.

But he wouldn't go out with Mom any more and point out rings only to be laughed at afterward, no sir. He went out alone and looked. From store to store.

At last he found a very pretty ring with a big pearl. The pearl was set in the middle of a little golden crown. That was just the ring for Mom.

But it cost more than twenty dollars.

And he didn't have a cent.

What should he do now?

Money was really a big problem. His piggy bank had been full for ages when he never needed a cent. Then suddenly he got rid of all his coins and now he needed them.

Is that how it always is with money?

Then he could understand why Mom and Dad talked about money all the time, as if they couldn't think of anything else. Now he could hardly think of anything else either.

He tried to count how much twenty dollars was. It took quite a while to count, so it was probably much too much.

But he shouldn't think that way! Mom was going to get that ring. And be happy.

Money wasn't going to stop him.

Because money was just bits of metal and paper, but a ring wasn't.

He had to talk to Dad again.

Of course, he probably could have talked with Grandad about it, or with Granny. They would surely have helped him make Mom happy. But first he would try Dad one more time. Because Mom would be happier if she got it from him.

If only he knew how to put it to him!

He mustn't pester him; he knew that perfectly well.

He started by sitting with Dad in front of the TV, watching ice hockey all one evening. He listened to Dad explain the game.

That put Dad in a good mood.

Then the next day he told Dad about the ring. But he didn't say that he wanted him to buy it; he just told him how pretty it was. And Dad listened.

That evening there was a match on TV again, and

Elvis sat there and discussed it. He remembered every little bit that Dad had taught him about ice hockey the evening before. Dad was in an even better mood.

Elvis didn't say a word about the ring.

The next day Dad went out and bought it. He thought that it was an unusually pretty ring too.

So then the surprise was all set for Mom.

Great! Then Elvis figured that he didn't have to watch any more ice hockey.

But a couple of evenings later, Dad shouted:

"Hurry up, Elvis! Ice hockey! Finland against Poland!"

Yes—there he sat again, because Dad's voice sounded so very happy.

And Miss Magnusson had said that. . . .

Yes, what did she actually say?

It didn't matter.

It was only the teacher talking.

No—he had to obey himself too.

CHAPTER

19

WHAT AN INCREDIBLY remarkable ring it was!

Elvis had to rush to the drawer where Dad had hidden it to take it out over and over again and have a look.

The little crown that the pearl sat in looked so real.

Just think if there really were such a tiny head to wear it! And such tiny kings! A whole country of such tiny people!

Suddenly it came to Elvis what that would be like. And then he told Annarosa about the country where Mom's ring came from. He could picture absolutely clearly what happened when the king of that country lost his crown. It happened by mistake.

They had promised the king an Alexander cake for Easter, but he didn't get one, not on Easter or the day after. They broke their promise, so the king had to get one himself.

But he didn't know how to bake. And he didn't

have any money. So he promised to give his crown to the person who baked the best Alexander cake.

Naturally everyone started baking cakes, all the bakers throughout the kingdom.

Then they hurried over to the castle with their cakes and happened to arrive all at the same time. This wasn't so good, because obviously the king couldn't taste all those cakes at once. He sat there, not knowing which one to choose. They all looked equally good.

"Take mine! Take mine!" shouted the bakers.

"No, mine! No, mine!" they shouted.

The king got all confused and the bakers started fighting. Then the king descended from his throne to separate and reconcile them. And that was when, in the middle of the fight, he lost his crown. He didn't notice it right away, because everyone was fighting all around him. They hit each other so hard that the whole castle shook and trembled.

Then a good while later he noticed that his head felt so light and strange. His crown was gone. Everyone started looking for it. They searched high and low but no one could find it.

And when the bakers realized that the king no longer had his crown, they didn't care which cake he chose, so they all immediately became friends once again.

They took their cakes and left. And since the king

couldn't pay, they decided they might just as well eat their cakes themselves, so they trooped out of the castle.

And there sat the king, alone and abandoned, without his golden crown and without even an Alexander cake. And no one cared about him.

They never found the crown.

A human being had stolen it, an ordinary human, a fisherman who owned a pearl, and the pearl fitted perfectly into the king's crown. The fisherman had known for ages that it would.

That was why the fight was the ideal moment for him to steal the crown. It worked out well because he was much too big for any of the tiny people to see him in their tiny world. All he had to do was rock and tilt the castle a little bit and hold his hand under it, and the crown rolled out into his hand. That was when the castle shook, but everyone there thought it was because they were fighting so wildly.

Yes, the crown was very easy to steal.

Then the fisherman placed his pearl in the king's crown and sold it to a jeweler, who made a ring out of it.

The ring cost more than twenty dollars and Elvis' mom was going to get it as a Christmas present. They had already bought it, Elvis and his dad, and it was in a drawer at home in a red box with gold on it, Elvis told Annarosa.

"Is that really true?" she asked.

Elvis nodded. And she believed him. Neither of them doubted the story, and Old Granny didn't even ask whether it was true when she heard about it. She just nodded and said:

"There, you see. You don't need TV to learn what's happening in the world. We all have so much more inside ourselves than we know."

"But it's a pity about the king," said Annarosa. "He should get his crown back."

"He'd much rather have had an Alexander cake," said Elvis.

This surprised Annarosa. And she wondered, because she would much rather have had the crown.

"As for me, I don't think the king is alive," said Old Granny. "This must have happened a long time ago."

"People who lived a long time ago can still be alive. What about you?" Annarosa said seriously.

Old Granny nodded—it was true, she had to agree.

"But I think the king got his Alexander cake in the end," she said. "I do indeed. That I do."

"Even though he couldn't pay for it?" Annarosa sounded doubtful.

"He learned how to bake one himself, of course," replied Old Granny. "You mustn't think he just sat there with his hands in his lap."

No, Elvis couldn't picture that either, not for a long time. And of course, that way he could have had just the kind of cake he wanted.

But anyway Mom was going to have her ring. Nothing would interfere with that. This year Mom was going to have a real Christmas! He had made up his mind.

Annarosa's family didn't do much about Christmas. Her mother and granny both worked, and Old Granny was only interested in other Christmases that had happened long ago.

That sounds fine, thought Elvis, because at his house they didn't talk about anything else.

Then just a couple of days before Christmas, he heard something awful.

Annarosa's granny suddenly said that she never dared look in a mirror on Christmas eve.

Because mirrors are supernatural then. Something happens to them when the candles are lit. All the people who are going to die during the new year appear with no heads in mirrors on Christmas eve.

"Now don't you fill the kids with such nonsense," said Annarosa's mother. "You know just as well as I do that's plain nonsense, silly old superstition."

Old Granny didn't believe in that either.

Superstition or not—Elvis and Annarosa looked at each other; they turned pale and dark-eyed with terror. What they heard was so terrible that they didn't even dare ask about it. They didn't make a sound.

Even though Elvis usually believed what Old Granny said, he couldn't get it out of his head.

Day and night the thought suddenly flew up inside him like a black bird of terror. He couldn't understand how everyone could be so happy about Christmas and celebrate it so cheerfully if it hid such a horror. They should be busy covering all the mirrors and watching out about lighted candles.

Maybe most people didn't know anything about it. He watched Mom and Dad carefully, and they didn't seem to know. They acted the same as always.

He didn't dare ask anyone. Probably those who didn't know shouldn't be told. Because the people who already knew certainly had no comfort to give.

He thought about Johan. Did Johan see himself headless in a mirror on the Christmas eve before he died? Did Elvis dare telephone and ask? But what if Granny and Grandad didn't know . . . ?

No, Elvis had to keep this to himself. After thinking

it all through, he definitely decided to keep quiet about it.

At the same time he felt a smoldering bitterness, a dull anger.

How could the world be so cruel?

Here were people going around suspecting no harm at all, lighting lots of candles, giving each other gifts, being happy, while evil lay in wait for them everywhere. Within their own homes. Quite a number of people were preparing for a Christmas when it might only mean that they would see lots of headless people in their mirrors.

Did it have to be this way?

Poor Mom! Poor people!

And he had always thought that supernatural things were beautiful—like when yellow sunflowers grew out of black seeds. . . .

But this was unnatural, abominable. . . .

Never before had Elvis experienced such weird days. They passed both much too slowly and much too fast. One moment he thought about the ring that Mom would receive. Then he got excited and eager. But then the next moment the terror struck within him again, and then everything good stopped short and fell apart. Then he thought he would never be happy again.

He had to avoid mirrors on Christmas eve. Because that was the only day that mattered; afterward the danger would be past. The best thing would be to hide the mirrors in the closet, but that was probably impossible. Mom couldn't manage without them.

The most difficult one to avoid would be the hall mirror, because they had to pass it all the time.

The day before Christmas, Mom glued a lot of sprightly Christmas elves on the mirror to make it look cheery. In Elvis' eyes this only made it look more sinister. Ominous. He couldn't take his eyes off it.

Then Mom came over and felt his forehead.

"You do feel very hot, honey!" she said. "Now don't you go and get sick just for Christmas!"

"No, I'm quite well," said Elvis, but his head felt like a boiling casserole.

Mom took his temperature anyway, to make sure, but he didn't have a fever.

"It's probably because he's so looking forward to his presents," she said later to Grandma over the telephone.

She was afraid that she would have to phone them not to come, but there was no reason to worry. They could all come tomorrow.

CHAPTER

20

CHRISTMAS EVE was beautiful. It snowed lightly and the streets were quiet.

The room smelled of hyacinths.

Elvis had planted the hyacinths in pots a long time ago, before he got to know Miss Magnusson and Anna-rosa, while he was still walking around, deciding whether to start school. Now they were blossoming—white, blue, pink.

A blue one was standing in front of the hall mirror. Elvis moved it; Mom put it back. Elvis went there again. Mom too.

"Now don't be silly, Elvis! The hyacinth is staying right here! See!"

"It'll be too dark for it," Elvis tried.

"Not at all," said Mom. "Soon we'll light the candles."

There was a candle on either side of the hyacinth. Everything was all prepared. Everything was moving forward, inexorably; there was nothing he could do. Except wait. . . .

Right after that, everyone arrived, Dad's parents and Mom's parents. And they all stood around for a while in the front hall by the mirror, but the candles weren't lit yet, so there was still no danger. Annarosa's granny said that the mirrors didn't become supernatural until the candles were lit.

Everyone had lots of packages; everyone was happy; and Grandad joked with Elvis as usual. He clearly knew nothing about the mirrors, and he usually knew almost everything. Up to the last moment, Elvis hoped that the two of them together could figure out a way to deal with the mirrors. But that was dumb because if Grandad knew, he would surely have done away with Christmas years ago.

No, Elvis had to get through it all by himself; he realized that no one could help him. The remarkable thing was that as soon as he really understood that, he suddenly became absolutely and totally calm. His head stopped feeling hot and throbbing. It turned cold instead.

"I think Elvis looks very pale," Grandma said to Mom.

"Yes, he does!" Mom answered in surprise. "A minute ago, he was red as a lobster. It must be the excitement. Kids are like that . . . they can get quite sick from excitement."

Mom looked at Elvis and nodded with satisfaction—how nice, she thought, when he behaves normally, like an ordinary child.

"You'll see, Santa will be here soon," she said, patting him on the cheek. "We'll just have something to eat first. . . . But then you'll see!"

Mom winked secretively, and Elvis said:

"How can Santa know when we've finished eating?"

He said that to play along and make Mom happy. And it worked. She winked and laughed and repeated what he said, "You wonder how Santa can know when we have finished eating . . . !"

Elvis looked at Grandad furtively, so that Grandad would know that Elvis was playing at being childish, because he knew that Elvis was doing it for his mom. Grandad smiled at him and nodded encouragingly.

Then it struck Elvis that, in fact, he did know exactly how to be and what to say and do to make Mom happy. It took so very little, such unbelievably simple things—why couldn't he do it a bit more often? Since she thought it was such fun. Actually all he had to do was play at being a bit childish—and stop being who he really was.

Since he obviously couldn't be himself at home anyway, why not act childish instead of making a nuisance of himself? That might be a better thing to do.

It was difficult not being able to be what he really

was—but as long as he couldn't anyway? He definitely ought to think about this a little more.

"You told Santa what time we'd finish eating when you phoned him," Elvis went on innocently.

Mom clapped her hands and winked at Dad.

"Right, I did! How could I forget that! You're not so dumb, Elvis!"

She gave him a little hug.

Darkness was falling now, slowly, outside the windows.

Mom went around lighting all the candles.

Elvis followed her hand holding the match—from candle to candle. In the window, on the TV, on the dining table.

He felt cold as ice inside.

They sat down around the dining table. Everyone was hungry and happy. They all talked at once and laughed loudly.

The table was loaded with food. The candles flickered. Platters and dishes were passed back and forth. Everyone complimented Mom on the Christmas dinner. That made her happy too.

But Elvis couldn't swallow a bite of food.

"You know all children are alike," said Mom. "We'll have to hurry with the presents before he starves to death."

They all laughed at that. Elvis too.

"If you knew what you were getting from Santa,

Mom, you'd starve too," he said, and Dad hushed him secretively.

Mom's cheeks turned red.

"What I'm getting from Santa?" she said in surprise. "I'm not getting anything! The main thing is that Santa is coming to you, Elvis."

"No, to you!" said Elvis.

"Oh, isn't he sweet!" Mom said, moved.

Elvis gave her a serious look but she didn't notice. Poor, poor Mommy. . . .

Now he knew the person he was most frightened of seeing in the mirror without a head was . . . Mom. Even though Granny and Grandad and Grandma and Grandpa were old and easier to imagine, still he wasn't worried about them. Or about Dad either, and hardly about himself.

No—he wasn't seriously worried about any of the others, just Mom, because in that case it would be his fault.

If something happened to Mom, he would be to blame.

He had thought so many terrible thoughts, said so many terrible things—even hit her—but the thoughts were probably the worst. . . .

So if anyone were going to appear without a head in the mirror that evening, it would be Mom! He realized that.

Ever since the candles had been lit and there was no turning back, he had also known that he wouldn't be able to get rid of the mirrors. The only thing to do was find out what was in them. Otherwise he'd worry about it all year long until the next Christmas eve.

It would be better to find out as quickly as possible. Then he'd know what to do. Because naturally he wasn't going to let anything happen to Mom. But first she had to have her real Christmas.

He had the whole evening before him. He could wait until Santa had come and gone, until Dad came back and everyone calmed down after they exchanged gifts. When they were all sitting around cracking nuts, he would go off for a while by himself and look in the hall mirror.

After the Christmas dinner Mom snuffed out the candles and lit the Christmas tree. Meanwhile Dad disappeared.

"I'm just going out to stretch my legs," he said. "I really need to after all that food."

"Yes, go ahead," Mom answered. "But hurry back so you'll be here before Santa comes."

"Yes, or Santa will be mad at you, and then you won't get any presents," said Elvis childishly.

"Is that so! Will Santa be mad at Dad?" said Mom, winking again.

Then Dad disappeared and returned as Santa and was very surprised to find that he himself wasn't home. Everyone thought it was such a shame.

"I could go look for him," said Elvis in that innocent way.

But Santa didn't want him to, and no one else did either.

"Dad will be back very soon," Mom said. She was having a hard time keeping from laughing.

Then Dad asked, "Are there any good children hereabouts?" in his Santa voice, looking at Elvis.

"I don't know," said Elvis frankly.

Then Santa turned to Mom.

"Well, I can't complain," she said. "Yesterday and today he has been really sweet."

Then they started giving presents.

Elvis got package after package; he broke the wrappings and took out the toys, but he hardly knew what he was doing and he didn't see what he got.

"Take it easy, Elvis," said Mom. "You're not really enjoying your presents that way. What will Santa think?"

"Right, Elvis, do what Mom says!" said Santa in Dad's voice; then his beard started to shake and he said in a deeper Santa voice than usual:

"Right—or Santa will get mad at you!"

They all laughed. But Elvis stared at him wide-eyed.

At that moment Mom opened a package from her mom.

"A makeup mirror!" she exclaimed. "How great!"

Elvis stood up and dropped what he was holding.

Mom was twisting and turning a round, two-sided mirror.

"It has a real mother-of-pearl handle," said

Grandma, "and that's a magnifying mirror on the other side."

"Yes, I see," said Mom. "It's really nice. . . ."

Elvis held his breath and stared at her. Had the time come? He had planned on waiting until after all the presents. But now Mom was lifting up the mirror to look in it.

No, not yet!

Elvis dashed over and grabbed the mirror out of her hand.

"Heaven's sake!" said Mom. "Can't I look in my own mirror?"

Everyone looked startled, but they laughed too because of course it was Christmas eve.

Elvis stood there with the mirror, not knowing what to do with it. But he couldn't stay like that with everyone staring at him.

So then he said, in that childish way, "We're going to look in it together, both of us."

"Yes, let's do that," said Mom delightedly, putting her arm around him.

He handed her the mirror again. Everyone smiled.

Mom rested the mirror on her knee and put her head against his. She leaned forward over the mirror.

Elvis' heart almost stopped beating and everything looked quite dark in front of his eyes.

He couldn't see anything. Mom moved the mirror slightly and hugged him.

"Now I see you," she said. "Can you see me?"

Elvis couldn't get a sound out. Everything looked bright and weird but he could see a face in the mirror —enormous, lit by the candles on the tree as they flickered and fluttered. The face beamed up at him, as unreal as a moon face.

"Are you looking in the magnifying side?" Grandma asked.

"Yes, you can imagine how funny Elvis looks!" Mom laughed.

Elvis sank down on the floor and was given another package to open.

He should be feeling calmer now—her head was in the mirror—but he wasn't. He didn't recognize Mom in the mother-of-pearl mirror. It might have been someone else. An optical illusion. Something supernatural, that much he could see. He still had to check it later in the hall mirror as he had planned.

That one was probably the most reliable.

Then Mom was given her fantastic present. Dad had wrapped the box in white paper with gold crowns on it and he had put a big gold bow on top.

Mom held it carefully.

Santa said that it was from Dad. Then he said that it was from Santa.

"Now then, who's it really from?" laughed Mom.

"From me!" said Santa.

"No! From Dad!" said Elvis.

Mom held the package and marveled at it. She

thought it was almost a pity to open it, but Santa said that what was inside was even finer, and Elvis nodded eagerly.

Then Mom opened the package slowly. When she saw the ring, she became totally quiet. She just stared and stared. A long time passed before she took it out of the box.

"Oh!" was all she said. "Oh!"

Then she picked it up. It fitted her perfectly, equally well on either ring finger.

"Oh!" she said again.

"Well, what do you think?" Santa asked with Dad's voice, but no one was bothering about that now.

Mom looked completely dazed.

"It's incredibly beautiful," she said, "but pearls . . . don't pearls mean tears?"

"Not that I know!" said Grandma.

"I think I've heard that," said Mom.

But everyone else said that was not to be taken seriously, it was just old-fashioned superstition that no one believed any more nowadays.

Santa scratched himself under his beard and said he didn't know.

"Elvis helped me," he said. "He was really the one who chose the ring and neither of us could have known that."

"I know," said Mom, "and it doesn't matter anyway."

But Elvis sat there, feeling cold in his heart.

What had he done now?

Everyone was saying how clever he was and what good taste he had and all sorts of things like that, but their voices sounded very distant, far, far away.

There seemed to be no end to the harm that he caused his mom. And now had he even chosen tears for her? He certainly did understand why she thought he was a punishment for her sins. . . .

He got up from the floor and disappeared out into the hall.

He might as well find out now once and for all.

"Elvis! Where are you off to?" Mom called.

He didn't answer. His voice wasn't working.

"What are you doing, dear?" she called.

The candles in front of the mirror weren't lit. Elvis took the matchbox that was there and lit them.

Mom came out into the hall after him.

"You're not allowed to light matches, you know that, Elvis dear," she said. "Besides, we're opening our presents now. . . ."

She stopped and stared at him.

He was standing there in front of the mirror with the blue hyacinth in his arms. She thought he was worrying about whether it was too dark for the hyacinth. She went over and stood beside him.

"Of course, we can light the candles out here," she said, "so you won't worry about the flowers. Put them back."

Then Elvis looked up and saw her in the mirror. She met his eyes and was quiet. His eyes had such a strange expression . . . so very solemn. And on Christmas eve!

Why was he looking like that?

Elvis looked at her steadily. Looked and looked. To make sure that he was seeing properly.

Yes—Mom's head was all there! She looked just the same. No illusion. No moon face. It was Mom's face all right.

Yes, everything was the same as always. He could see that now. There was nothing supernatural. Not even the ring on Mom's finger, though it was still unusually beautiful.

The only supernatural thing was—of course, just as he always thought—the blue hyacinth. Everything else was a lot of dumb talk.

"Let's not stay out here, Elvis," said Mom. "We still have lots of presents to open. We can't keep Santa waiting. . . ."

Elvis put the hyacinth back between the candles in front of the mirror and went back with Mom to join the others.

He discovered that Grandad had given him a tool chest! Wow! And there was a construction set from Grandpa! And heaps of other things!

This was really fun!

Suddenly he turned to Mom and threw his arms around her.

She didn't have to die just because the two of them didn't get on. How could he ever have thought that? They couldn't help it, either of them. They liked each other anyway. Now he knew that.

CHAPTER

2 1

WELL, CHRISTMAS EVE was over now, it would be a long time to the next one, and everyone was still sleeping.

And to think that Elvis had been so frightened!

Of nothing!

Now he knew—you can be frightened of nothing at all.

Mom and Dad were still sleeping in their beds, but Elvis got up and watered the hyacinths. He came out of the bathroom with his watering can and suddenly found a beam of sunlight.

The sun thresholds!

The sun was shining on the thresholds again! Sunlight was pouring into the room, the whole room was golden, it was as if honey were glowing in the air. It was supernaturally beautiful and good, he knew that for sure. . . .

He took the hyacinths and lined them up on the threshold where the sun shone most brightly, because they should have a good time too.

Then he got dressed and ran outside. It would be quite a while before they woke up today. He hurried so that he would be sure to meet Annarosa and get back again. He wanted to hear how her Christmas eve had been.

There was quite a lot of snow outside because it had snowed all night long.

He could hear laughter in Annarosa's courtyard from a long way off. They were shoveling snow in there and throwing snowballs at each other. Annarosa and her mom and granny and a stranger too. He threw a snowball at Elvis as soon as he saw him.

Elvis threw one back.

A hit! The man's cap fell off!

But he just laughed and included Elvis in the snowball game.

Then Elvis heard them call the man—Enar.

Could this be Enar, drunken Enar? Annarosa was so scared that he might show up on Christmas eve. He had threatened to, and had already ruined several Christmases for them before. So surely this was another Enar, because this one was really happy and fun and made everyone else happy too.

Time just flew by—and Elvis had to be back home before they woke up. Suddenly he remembered and ran home as fast as he could.

Luckily they hadn't had time to get angry yet. They were just out of bed and seemed very surprised to find the hyacinths on the threshold.

"I almost walked right into them," said Mom.

"They are supposed to get some sunshine, that was why I put them there," explained Elvis.

Dad looked out the window and said that the sun wasn't shining today.

No, not any longer; Elvis could see that too, but there had been sunshine, the whole room had been golden with sunshine.

"Then why didn't you put the hyacinths on the windowsill? That's where people put flowers," Mom said.

"There was much more sun on the threshold, you see. . . ."

Both Mom and Dad started laughing. They thought that he had been dreaming and walked in his sleep and put the hyacinths on the threshold then. That would have been fun to see, they said.

"You and your bright ideas," said Dad.

"You said it!" said Mom.

She was wearing the ring and now she looked at it and said that Elvis had such good taste. Just imagine, he made such a good choice!

But she didn't know which hand to wear it on—the left or the right. It would be better on her left hand, she thought, but you could see it better on her right, the one she put out to shake hands.

Well, Elvis didn't know which was best. Nor did Dad.

"You can ask your friends," said Elvis. "They'll know for sure."

But Mom thought none of her friends would phone until the holidays were over, everyone was usually busy over Christmas. So Mom had to wait to decide which hand to wear the ring on.

"Unless you figure it out yourself," said Dad.

But Mom didn't think she could; she wanted to hear what the others thought first.

After they had eaten, Elvis went out again. And no one said anything about it, because it was Christmas, so no one stopped him. They knew that he wanted to be out in the snow.

"Just don't come home too late," said Mom. "And remember it'll get dark early."

"Yes, listen to what Mom is telling you, Elvis," said Dad.

"Right," said Elvis.

He was going to meet Annarosa again. They were going to build snow lanterns to put candles inside.

"Shall we start in your yard or mine?" asked Annarosa.

"Yours!" answered Elvis, because it wasn't a very good idea for Annarosa to come home with him because of his mom.

But it turned out that Annarosa didn't want to be in her yard today.

"Why do we always have to be over at my place all the time?" she asked.

Elvis didn't answer that, because he couldn't tell her what his mom had said, that he wasn't allowed to spend time with Annarosa. Instead he suggested that they make snow lanterns somewhere completely different, not in either yard where hardly anyone could see them. No, they should choose places that really needed them, so there'd be some point to them.

She thought that was a good idea. Secret places are always the best.

It had started snowing again, and only a few people were outside.

Elvis suddenly thought of Enar.

Were there really two—one Enar who got drunk and ruined Christmases and another who was nice and fun and threw snowballs?

"No, it's the same one," said Annarosa. "No one can believe it, but it's true."

Elvis had a hard time working it all out.

Weren't they going to move to another town because of Enar?

Weren't they scared of him and of opening their door in case he was there?

Didn't they want to get rid of him forever?

"But that's only when he's drunk," said Annarosa, "that's the only time he acts dumb."

But Johnny was dumb all the time, even though he never drank.

"And that's much worse," she said.

Elvis thought so too, much worse.

"So now your mom is going to marry Johnny?" he asked.

Annarosa shook her head.

No, that was all over. Johnny had come over to the house and buttered her up a lot and been extra specially boring and now he had only himself to blame. Enar made fun of him; Mom too. Besides, Annarosa had never liked Johnny. He was stuck up and a show-off and he thought he could decide everything.

"For us, can you imagine?" she said, looking at Elvis. "Isn't that dumb?"

Yes, Elvis agreed, incredibly dumb. He liked Enar better; but of course, he'd only seen the fun side of him; he could hardly imagine the drunken side.

"So then he doesn't drink all the time?" he asked.

No, only sometimes. And now he'd probably stay sober for a couple of months, Annarosa's mother thought, because now they were together again. Yesterday, on Christmas eve, they suddenly made up. He came over with presents for everyone and hadn't had anything to drink. But they didn't know until then that he had got over his drinking, which was why they were scared, because usually he really got going with his drinking just for Christmas. It was like a sickness, but now he was healthy for a while and everything was just fine. They had a happy Christmas.

"It was almost like having my own dad," said Annarosa.

For that matter, perhaps he was her dad; she almost
believed it, she hoped so, when he was nice like this.
But when he was drunk, she didn't want him, and
Mom didn't want anything to do with him either.

"But if he is really sick . . . ," said Elvis.

"Yes, it's really too bad," Annarosa said, and both of
them sighed at the thought of what a good dad Enar
would be if he didn't drink.

It was all new to Elvis and hard for him to understand—though not impossible to imagine—that one
human being could be two very different people.
There was an explanation somewhere for most everything. He knew that now.

"So are you going to move?" he asked.

She didn't think so, not for a while anyway, not
until Enar started drinking again.

"Perhaps he's stopped for good," said Elvis, "and
won't ever start again."

But she didn't think that he could control himself
like that, not his whole life long. Still, while it lasted,
they'd have a good time with him.

They were just crossing a street at a wide intersec-
tion.

"Here!" said Elvis, stopping suddenly.

"What?" Annarosa stopped too.

"We'll make our first snow lantern here!"

Right in the middle of the crossroads! Where the four streets met! What a strange idea! She looked at him quite alarmed.

"But this isn't a secret place!"

"Sure it is!"

"No, not when everyone can see it!"

"Yes, that's exactly why! That's exactly the point. . . ."

Of course, everyone should be able to see the snow lanterns, but no one would ever guess who built them. The two of them would be the only ones who knew.

"So it'll be secret anyway," explained Elvis.

Annarosa didn't really go along with that; she looked at the spot hesitantly. There weren't very many cars on the roads then, but there would be soon and they'd drive right into the snow lantern and knock it down. Didn't he realize that?

"You know it'll get run over," she said.

"No." Elvis didn't think so. Everyone would be happy when they saw it so they'd be careful. This was the very spot that needed a snow lantern. Couldn't she see that?

Annarosa didn't say anything more to contradict him. Though she was still a bit dubious, she got right to work helping, when Elvis started making snowballs. They needed a tremendous lot of them because it was going to be a big lantern, but there was plenty of snow and the work was easy and fun.

"Then we'll make some more, okay?" she asked.

"Obviously," Elvis answered. "And we'll find really good places."

Soon the snow lantern was finished.

Annarosa had brought along some candles.

She asked, "Which of us should light it?"

"You—if you like," said Elvis.

She chose one of the candles and stood it up inside the lantern.

"My lucky candle, that Old Granny gave me," she said, lighting it as Elvis added the last snowballs to close off the top.

Old Granny had given her matches too.

"She trusts us, you see," she said. "I promised to use them only for the snow lanterns."

Elvis nodded.

"See?" he said.

Yes, she did—the cars slowed down and swung out of the way of the snow lantern, just as Elvis thought they would. And it really glowed and they could see it from a long way off from every direction. Yes, it was absolutely the right place, no doubt about it.

"Shall we look for a new place now?" she asked eagerly.

"I'm just going to look at the lantern for a little while," said Elvis.

Annarosa handed him a square snowball.

"Fix this one for me?" she asked.

As Elvis rounded it into shape, thoughts sped through his head, in and out like gusts of wind.

What a difference between now and before, between this and last Christmas, between being alone and being. . . .

He looked at Annarosa—the shadows and the light from the snow lantern flickered over her face, like dark and light butterflies. Just like his thoughts, they fluttered like butterflies too between then and now.

You don't have to be sad because you are alone—but *if* you are, then you feel like nobody at all.

But when you're happy as he was right then, you feel more than double yourself. . . .

He looked at Annarosa again. . . .

She was making another snowball, which wasn't going to turn out round either, and she looked back at him and laughed. No one had ever looked at him like that; she was the only one, always, right from the start.

"Pack this one for me?" she asked.

Elvis handed her the snowball he had finished making and took her square one. He looked around while he packed this one for her too—here, all around them, was the world, white and wide, limitless; he could wander off in any direction and build more snow lanterns. So many were needed, everywhere in fact. . . .

They smiled at each other. . . . Annarosa had started another snowball, which she wasn't making properly either. Elvis took it and handed her the one that was fixed.

"I'll pack this one for you," he said.

His thoughts flew.

He said suddenly, "Together a person is four!"

At first she didn't understand him at all.

He had to explain it to her. It was a question of counting, and actually she was better at that than he was, but this time he had to help her count.

They counted on their fingers and added them together.

Yes—it was right. Now she understood!

"I have myself, right? And I have you. . . .

"Then you have you, and you have me.

"So that's two for you and two for me—

"Then each two is one that's you and one that's me—"

"Two plus two!"

"Exactly! Together a person is four!"

They counted right.

MARIA GRIPE

recently won the highest international award in children's literature, the Hans Christian Andersen Medal. This award was given in recognition of the universal appeal of her books, which have now been translated into thirteen languages. Her much-loved HUGO AND JOSEPHINE trilogy won her both the Astrid Lindgren Prize and the Nils Holgersson Plaque, the most important Scandinavian prize for children's books, and was also made into a film.

Maria Gripe is now engaged in adapting some of her stories for Swedish television. She lives in Sweden, with her husband Harald Gripe, an artist who has illustrated most of her books, and her daughter Camilla, also a writer.